Femme Fatale

FEMME FATALE

RUBY SMOKE

*To those in the LGBTQIA+ Community who feel underrepresented,
we don't belong in a box. Fuck the box. Let's rebuild the mold, because
we are here and we aren't going anywhere.
This is for you.*

Welcome to Femme Fatale, an exclusive pleasure club where women can indulge their deepest desires.

The owner? Josslyn, a succubus who knows just how to captivate and satisfy her female patrons.

When Adelaide and Karissa enter the interview process, Joselyn never expects to be so captivated by the two of them. They quickly become her obsession, and she can't help but want to make them hers'.

As Adelaide and Karissa learn the ropes of Femme Fatale, they too can't help but feel an intense connection to Joselyn.

They want to be her sweet obsession just as much as she wants them to be.

But they soon realize that having Josslyn means having to have each other in every way possible.

This is just the beginning...

The cast is ready to welcome you..
will you join them?

Copyright

Author's Note

Femme Fatale is where you can live out all your female/female desires. Ever wondered, even briefly, how another female would make you feel intimately? If so, this book is for you. Within these pages, you can live out your fantasies and explore that urge you keep hidden. However, within Femme Fatale, there is no need to hide. We see you.

❖

Every inch of this book will be very explicit with a touch of magic, intrigue, and mystery. So if that is not your cup of tea, turn back now. If it is, grab a toy and some batteries.

Welcome to FEMME FATALE.

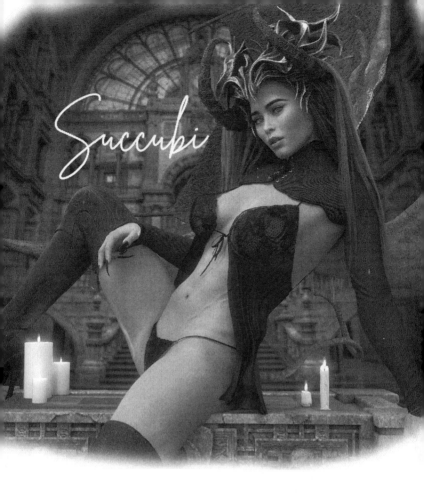

Succubi

Succubi are a curious type of creature. Although "creature" may put their status at a disadvantage. A more accurate title would be "Demon." More specifically, a Lilian-demon that is said to appear in the dreams of men to seduce them. Repeated sexual activity can usually drain said men's life force, rendering them physically and mentally unstable until the man ceases to exist.

But men are weak. Men fall prey to seduction. Women, however, wield seduction as a weapon. Women's unique femininity has driven men to the brink of insanity for thousands of years and will continue to do so. The art of seducing a man is no challenge at all. But the seduction and pleasure of a woman? Now that holds its own power. The skill set needed to bring pleasure to a woman in numerous ways requires training both in sexual pleasure and mental fortitude. The art of seducing a woman will forever be intricate as well as awe-inspiring. The art will take women from being sexual beings to being sexually free. At Femme Fatale, the line is toed between sexual freedom and divine—although demonic in nature—soul-shattering pleasure. Whatever your womanly desire, Femme Fatale is there to cater to those whims, and the Succubus on site is said to be the most efficient when drawing pleasure from all of her patrons throughout time.

JOSSLYN

I LEAN BACK ON THE COUCH IN MY OFFICE, HOLDING A HEAD between my thighs. I moan as I grip the girl's hair, gyrating my hips up, riding her face. One perk of being *the* boss... very hands-on interviewing. The women who work at Femme had certain... predilections... whether that is being submissive, dominant, or someone who can take the body through the thin line between pain and pleasure.

Are you confident enough in your sexuality to help

someone live out their fantasy? Can you give someone the illusion of power? Do you know how to wield dominance to maximize physical and emotional pleasure? Most importantly, have you embraced the unique power of your sensuality? Body type doesn't matter, but sex appeal? Confidence? Absolutely. We have a reputation to maintain, and I will interview the fuck out of everyone, literally, until they fit the bill. I am down two girls this summer and these two think they have what it takes to be a Fatale. I will certainly know soon.

"Fuck yes," I groan as she expertly sucks and flicks my clit, alternating her tempo. Leaving one hand wrapped in her hair, I reach up to bring the fat ass of the other girl riding my face closer. Best friends, I think. I didn't bother catching too many details, but their applications were solid, and their STD tests came back clean. They are both gorgeous and, even better, just my type—thick and with pouty lips that belong wrapped around my clit. *The one between my legs is doing an excellent job*, I think as I moan, my hips jerking with her renewed vigor. I may have to book this one for a few private shows myself.

I focus my attention on the plump ass on my face as I swirl my tongue around her clit, letting my piercing tease her. She throws her head back and moans as I take her clit between my lips and suckle. I look up at her in the throes of passion and lust shoots down my spine as I take in her perfect breasts, plump pussy, thick thighs, the small curve of her belly, and her body covered in tattoos. When she throws her head back, her curly hair tumbles down her back.

Reaching up to cup her own breasts, she moans my name in a thick Spanish accent as she shakes.

"Yes, Josslyn," echoes around the room. I prefer when applicants call me boss, but I can forgive the slip. Maybe.

Closing my thighs around the girl's head between my legs to hold her in place, I reach up to grab the Latin girl's ass, pushing her pussy firmly down onto my lips as I work her into a frenzy. Her moans become longer, her accent more pronounced, as she curses and tries to pull away from my onslaught. Holding back a grin at the effect I have on women, I grab her thighs, wrapping them firmly around my face, working her clit over until she screams my name and begs me to stop. I chuckle as I grab on more firmly to keep her in place as I continue to lap her up. She looks down at me, her face flush, her lips plump from biting them, and she reaches for my head to try to get me to stop. I shoot her a warning glare that would have most people running. Her eyes dilate even more as she instead grabs my hair and rides my face harder. She screams as she comes, her juices pouring down my neck. She whimpers as I hold her in place, my eyes rolling back as her friend works an orgasm out of me. I moan as I tighten my thighs, keeping her face in place while the last of my orgasm shudders throughout my body.

I shift the girl off the top of my face, settle her on the floor and sit on her face, her hands gripping my plump ass with excitement as she licks me from ass to clit. I shudder, still sensitive, and turn to reposition the other girl on the couch to settle myself between her thick, mocha thighs, now perfectly on display in front of me. I run my fingers lightly across her pussy, noting how wet she is, and blow across her clit. She moans in excitement before my tongue even touches her, and I grin.

I reach up to caress her heavy breasts and tweak her nipples between my fingers while grinding my pussy on the face of the girl beneath me. I hiss in pleasure as she opens my cheeks and concentrates her attention on my asshole. Focusing back on the girl in front of me, my eyes snap to attention as she arches her back, her beautiful chocolate breasts with pink nipples on display, and I curse. Fuck, she is gorgeous. I stand up, repositioning myself directly on top of her, kissing her pouty lips deeply. Running my tongue across hers, I brace myself with one hand near her head and bring my other hand around to apply pressure to her throat. Her eyes widen and roll back as she instinctively starts moving her hips against my stomach to alleviate the building pressure. With one last lick, I make my way down to draw her nipple into my mouth, alternating between sucking, biting, and licking, keeping her squirming.

"Please," she moans throatily, and I chuckle.

"What's your name again, sweetie?" I ask, reaching between her legs, and working two fingers into her tight pussy, curling my fingers to touch her sweet spot. I already know, but in the throes of passion, you have to be able to answer some basic questions. I trail kisses along her pelvic bone, avoiding where she desperately wants me. She cries out and rolls her hips, seeking more. I slow down and frown. I like my questions answered.

"Her name is Adelaide, and I'm Jaime," her friend responds for her. I scowl.

"I didn't ask you, I asked her." I reach back and grab Jaime by her head and position her face between my ass. "Now eat this pussy from the back and I might make you come again tonight." Jaime moans and gets on all fours, licking my slit with enthusiasm. *She isn't as good as Adelaide, but she has a gift for sure*, I think as I push my ass back, accepting her onslaught. I focus back on the girl in front of me. She is submissive, and we need a submissive Femme for our more... enthusiastic members. *Don't get me wrong, abuse isn't tolerated... much*. Just enough to bring pleasure to the customer and the Femme. In truth, that is why "Femme" was a thing of beauty—women understand women.

"Adelaide, do you want to cum?" I ask, focusing back on her sweet, innocent look.

She whimpers, as I draw close to her slit and lick softly.

"Answer me," I demand.

"Yes, please, yes."

I smile as I take ahold of her thighs, wrap them around my head and push my face right where it belongs, sucking her clit between my lips, flicking it unmercifully with my tongue. I groan as Jaime leans in and grabs my thighs, sucking my clit between her teeth, and gently biting down.

I switch my attention back to Adi who is bucking from me, switching up my speed, while still pushing my ass back into Jaime.

"I'm gonna cum!" she screams. I feel her clench her thighs as her cream drips down my chin. With her still breathless, I switch positions. Lying my head back on the couch, shoving my hand into Jaime's hair and moving her to face my pussy from the front, I firmly hold her in place with my thighs. I crook my finger at Adelaide and have her place her knees on either side of my head. I run my hands over her soft body, smacking her ass before getting a firm grip and settling her onto my face. I suck her clit between my lips, swirling my tongue slowly across the swollen nub. She curses, reaching for the back of the couch but then changes her mind as she wraps her hands into my hair, grinding herself onto my tongue, throwing her head back. The way she holds my head, arches her back, and pushes her breasts forward are magic. A little of both with this one, and so fucking sweet. I focus my mouth on her pussy while my eyes take in her curves and her pouty mouth as it opens and moans.

"Yes-s, pl-lease," she stutters out. I begin working my face harder as I grab her thighs, pressing them tightly across my face. I restrict her movement while running my tongue up and down her slit, drawing out her pleasure, but not letting her get her release. Smacking her ass, I push her off. "Turn around, now."

She quickly turns, her ass now in my face, in reverse. *So*

fucking perfect, I think as I grab her hips and press her back down against my lips. I alternate eating her ass and running my hands up the curve of her back and gripping her hair. She has free rein and is rolling my nipples between her soft hands. I moan into her pussy as her friend picks up her pace, drawing my clit between her lips. I grab Adelaide's ass hard, making her shift forward, her hands falling against my hips. Picking up on the hint, she and Jaime share a kiss over my pussy, before Adelaide leans down and licks my slit, taking turns with Jaime. I bite back a yell as they make me cum and I smack Adelaide's ass as a treat. Pushing her off me, I stand, taking in both of their lusty expressions, and smile.

Final test, I think, although this is definitely one of the best interviews I have held. "Turn around, Adelaide, and get on your knees. I want to watch you eat Jaime out. Taste her pussy for me like a good girl." I lean over and whisper into her ear, smiling as she immediately turns around and does what I said. As I take in the sight before me—Jaime moaning as she grips Adelaide's head—I slip on a special harness I had made that goes inside of me and vibrates on my clit. It has an attachment to fuck as well that feels fleshy. This shit is amazing. But there is something about grabbing a fat ass and a small waist and working it over with a dick I don't technically have, that just turns me on.

I waste no time as I position myself behind her plump, light mocha ass and pink pussy before slamming my manufactured nine inches deep inside of her. She screams a muffled "yes" from between Jaime's legs, but I am lost as I grip her hips firmly and roll and work my hips. I fuck her, effectively pushing her face harder into Jaime, who is screaming out her orgasm but still holding Adelaide firmly between her thighs. Yeah, she is that good. I want to keep her there, too. I lean over her, placing soft kisses onto her back, reaching under to play with her clit while I fuck her gently. She groans, pushing back, and I lightly smack her ass. The one right here is someone I can see myself keeping around. Fuck, she is so perfect. There is immediate sexual attraction, but then there is sexual dynamite. This is dynamite.

She comes with a loud scream and I slip out, remove my harness, and go to step back into my suit while they try to get their bearings back.

"You ladies are hired. Report back tomorrow for training." I smile and go to the washroom in my office to freshen up, wash my face, and reapply my lipstick. When I step back into the office, the girls are on their way out.

"Oh, and Adelaide?"

She pauses at the door, biting her lip, her shirt a little misshapen.

I slip her one of my cards. "Practice makes perfect," I whisper, leaning over to adjust her shirt. I wink and close the door.

❖

Earlier in the day
Adelaide

We stand outside of Femme Fatale, ready, or at least as ready as we can be, for our hands-on interview.

When Jaime came home the other day, bouncing on her

toes in excitement, I knew things were about to change for us. Call it intuition or the fact that we had been struggling for months to make ends meet while we juggled school and dead-end jobs.

"I got us interviews for Femme Fatale!" she screeched as she started tossing me clothes from the closet.

"Quick, throw something on. We have to go do a full panel STD screening for our interview next week."

A set of yoga pants hit my face as I pushed myself out of bed, still exhausted from working at the ratty dive bar all night and pushing hands off me. "How did you manage that?"

Femme Fatale is the city's best high-end female "escort", which everyone figures really meant sex, club. Only the most exclusive clients are reputed to go there—top female politicians, CEOs and the like. Hell, it is rumored it's taken years to come off their waitlist and is owned by the most ruthless woman in the state.

"Well, two of the girls that used to work there, I heard from a friend of a friend…" I raised my eyebrows as I pulled on my pants. "Okay, okay," she amended. "I was eavesdropping at the bar yesterday and heard that two of the girls ended up falling in love with one of the clients. I ran over after my shift and asked the bouncer if we could interview."

"Ah, that explains why I came home alone last night. I was wondering where you ran off to." I made my way into our tiny, shared bathroom and brushed my teeth, not bothering with makeup as I planned to throw myself back into bed after this test. I would be stupid not to go. This was a way to change our lives, to finally get things right. Besides, I never said no to Jaime. She had shown me true friendship, love and helped me realize who I really was. No, I was going to make sure we did this right.

I snap myself out of my thoughts and sigh. "I am a little nervous. What if she doesn't like us?"

Jaime scoffs and grabs my face. "Not possible and we don't do self-doubt. So let's go in there and kill it."

Nodding imperceptibly, I steel myself. *No self-doubt.* Jaime taught me everything I know, taught me who I am. I owe it to her, to both of us, to make this work.

Chapter Two

KARISSA

"Are you sure you're not a lesbian?" Daniel rolls his eyes and rolls away from me, grunting as his hand wraps around his length. "You hardly ever fucking kiss me, for God's sake, Rissa let alone fuck me..."

Sighing, I pinch the bridge of my nose as the beginnings of a headache begins to pound at my temples. "I don't know, Daniel. We've had this conversation so many times, I've lost count." I inch closer to him, trying to make it up to him somehow. "I-I can try again. Let me just try again."

I hate the pleading notes in my voice, but fuck, despite all the stress from this relationship, the times his anger got the best of him and he took it out on me, he really is all I have right now.

I hold back the tears and reach for him, only to be shoved

off him and onto the floor. Here it comes… Staying as still as I can, I wait for the barrage of hurtful words, the venom in his voice, and probably a few well-placed hits as well.

"Get out." The soft calm in his voice chills the blood in my veins.

"Danny," I start softly, raising my hands in surrender. "I can tr-try, baby. We can ma-make this work." Hell, who am I kidding? I doubt my words more than he does. I don't feel any sexual attraction to him. I do what I have to, to make this relationship work and I'm pretty sure he only puts up with it because of my looks. The son of a prominent political figure needs a girlfriend who would fit every aspect of his life, after all. Except, I couldn't do it sexually.

He whirls around to face me, the face that I once trusted during my weakest times, a mask of anger and fury. Gone is the All-American boy who'd given me hope that maybe I'm not the person I feel inside, the person my parents rejected and called unnatural. In his place is the green-eyed monster. "No. You know how many times you've said you would make it work? You're hot as hell, Karissa, but it's like fucking a curvy statue. You don't get wet, you don't like when I eat your pussy, hell, putting my dick inside of you makes me soft now. I like my women willing, and I'm tired of fucking some whore every night when I come back to this shit. Get the fuck out. Now."

I don't bother hiding the shock from my face. He's been fucking other people? Shit, I may not have been the best girlfriend but even I didn't cross that line. I may have been weak when I first came down, but I wasn't so far gone to plead when he clearly felt the need to betray me like this. So, I get the fuck out with nothing but the clothes on my back, cell phone, and a sudden sense of calm and freedom.

Walking down the dark street, I palm my phone and consider my options. I have a cousin who lives nearby. I know because I saw her from a distance once when I was on a date with Daniel. I had hidden my face and looked away, not knowing if she felt the same way as my family back home. I haven't spoken to her in years, but it's late, dark and I need help. I pray to the God that hasn't helped me in years, and look through my contacts before pressing the little phone icon, letting the phone ring.

"Chloe here." Her soft voice comes through the phone, music in the background.

"Chloe, it's Karissa. I know we haven't spoken in a while but I live close by and I really need help…" I hide the sound of regret from my voice as best as I can but I know it's still there.

She sighs softly, but I can tell it's a sound of relief rather than exasperation. "Drop me your location pin and I'll be there right away." I can hear faint notes of heavy bass music and wonder mutely where she is. I don't want to take her away from a party. "Just give me a few and let me talk to the boss lady."

The call disconnects, and I look down at my phone, sending her my location as I find a clean bench in this pristine neighborhood and sigh. Something is telling me I am about to start the rest of my life tonight.

❖

T he ride back to her work is quiet, yet comfortable, each of us lost in our thoughts. My voice seems loud in the car as I finally speak. "Thank you, Chloe. I didn't know who else to call, what else to do…"

The strawberry-blonde smiles across the console at me and pats my hand, her catlike green eyes so piercing that I feel like she is looking into my very soul. "We're family, Rissa, we look out for each other." I'm not sure how true that is, considering my own parents, but I'm glad she feels that way. I'm grateful to her and I say as much.

"Don't sweat it. I knew you moved here a while ago from the family grapevine. But after hearing what happened, I figured you would reach out to me when you were ready. I'm pretty much another black sheep in the family. My stepsister is the only one who still talks to me." She shrugs, tapping her fingers on the steering wheel.

After hearing what happened, suddenly, I am shoved into a memory.

"Karissa, your parents aren't home. They are still at the church event. Stop making excuses and lift that prissy dress. I've been waiting all week," my best friend, Lacey, demanded, pushing me up against the wall, kissing my neck. Pushing her hands under the top of my church dress, she grabbed my full breasts and groaned deeply.

"You said we weren't going to do this anymore, Lacey. It's not natural for us to do this." I bit back a moan as she took my nipple into her mouth and bit down.

"I lied. You want this, I want this, and I'll be damned if I look at you at school, in that graduation gown, knowing I could have had that sweet pussy in my mouth today." She looked at me sharply before grabbing me, turning me around, and shoving me onto the bed. I knew we should have stopped the first time this happened. After the tenth time, I knew I would be going to hell. Lacey and I had been best friends for years, but once we reached puberty, our sleepovers had much more tension than carefree fun. Our hand-holding in the pews while we sang started to mean more. One sleepover, I woke up with her tongue between my thighs and the most pleasure I had ever felt. Even though I tried to push her away, she held my hips down until my pleasure peaked. I bit my tongue to avoid waking my parents as she pushed my sleep gown further up and placed kisses all over my body, taking my breast into her mouth.

For a year, she touched me whenever she could. Sometimes we would go so far as to leave class early so she could lift my skirt up underneath the bleachers while everyone was in class. I'd even tasted her a couple of those times. She was much more aggressive and my lips would be swollen from her pushing her pussy into my face, but she preferred to go down on me. We were graduating tomorrow, and I was leaving to go on a college tour. We wouldn't see each other for a while.

Lifting my dress, she hurriedly pulled my panties off and curled her lips around that sweet spot. I clutched her head and moaned appreciatively. She groaned as she shoved her tongue inside of me, grabbing my waist as my back arched in pleasure.

"That's it, baby. Show me how much you're going to miss coming in my mouth," she growled. I came so hard I saw stars.

"What the fuck is this?" my father's voice boomed into the room.

It's been five years that instead of the college tour, I was kicked out and took some of my savings, and moved to Washington. I took all my transcripts, applied for financial aid, and went to Washington State University. Lacey, apparently, was sent to a church camp to repent. At least living on campus, I was free. I met Daniel soon after and decided that I would strive to live right, to put my past behind me. Unfortunately, it looked like although I could leave Texas, my true self followed me. Why can't I bring myself to want Daniel, to be sexually attracted to him—or any man? What is wrong with me?

Slamming my head down into my hands, I sigh. "Yeah, I'm not surprised you heard. It was the scandal of the lifetime in that small town."

"Don't do that, Karissa. I left because I knew I was different from the image they wanted. You may have been kicked out first, but I left soon after. It's time for you to accept who you are. I am going to help you," she says firmly, pulling up to a golden gate with the letters *FF* in script. There is security outside and a low thumping coming from what looks like a huge black mansion with gold trim. The top floor looks to be all windows that overlooks the property.

My jaw drops. "What is this place?"

"Club Femme Fatale. The start of your new life and self-discovery." A small smirk tilts her lips as she gets out and comes around to my side of the car. Helping me to stand, she spends a minute or two adjusting my clothes and fluffing my hair to "unleash my inner sex goddess," as she puts it. Even as I roll my eyes at her antics, I already feel much better. Sure, I still wear my favorite pair of ripped skinny jeans and a hoodie, but somehow I feel sexier than I have in a long time… invincible.

"Exactly where I think you need to be." She hugs me tightly. "We've got this girl."

I feel my face light up as I follow her past the gates and into the building.

My eyes bug out of my head as Chloe leads me past a huge foyer turned dance floor, and to an even larger room with plush chairs, dark walls, and wall-to-wall bars. At the side of the bar that Chloe goes behind as she tucks her car keys into what looks like a little locker is a hulking beast of a man. He is ripped, arms bulging across his chest. Definitely security for the place. The grin on his face is warm as he stands, and I have to crane my neck up to see his face. "Chloe the cat!" He lifts her off the ground in those great tree trunk arms of his before his eyes finally find mine. "Did you bring me a toy?"

Chloe scowls and slaps him soundly across the back of the head. "No, dipshit. This is my cousin. And even if you did like women, she's off-limits. Don't make me kick your ass." Laughter dances in her eyes as she smooches his cheek.

He scoffs. "You and Joss both. To be surrounded by beautiful women and not feel an inkling of desire for them… Still, men wish they were me."

I cock my head in confusion but before I can ask, Chloe continues with a smile, "Benny boy, this is Karissa. Rissa, this is Ben. He runs security around this joint." As if I hadn't guessed.

She wiggles out of his arms and stands—a little person compared to the seemingly seven-foot-tall giant. "Boss Lady still here?" At his nod, she takes a deep breath and grabs a few bottles, mixing me a drink. I turn around in my seat as they talk for a bit and take note of the various, beautiful, scantily clad, yet still sophisticated women I somehow missed when I walked in, working the room full of... women. I feel my jaw unhinge and Chloe chuckles as she comes around and presses a glass into my hand. "Welcome to heaven on earth, baby girl."

JOSSLYN

I LEAN BACK IN MY CHAIR, LOOKING THROUGH THE FINANCIAL records for the past quarter. I sigh. We are growing and doing well. The waitlist to join the club has me wondering if I should look into expanding the club. The two girls who were interviewed earlier are a good start, but I may need to look into adding another girl. Someone who can toggle between being submissive and dominant. Someone who, with a little training, could be the perfect lover and friend. Keep their clients coming back all day long for more. We may focus on physical pleasure, but the pleasure of the mind is just as important.

I lift my head as a tentative knock sounds from the door. "Come on in." I raise my voice, shuffling the papers on my desk and locking them in the drawer to my left before I acknowledge the girl in front of me.

I look up and smile warmly when I notice Chloe, one of our

best bartenders and hardest workers I have had the pleasure of employing. She balances bartending on some nights as well as having her own set of patrons. She doesn't have to, but she loves working behind the bar, her easy smile, and sassy attitude are the perfect way to ease the most nervous of clients into an easy rhythm. In short, she is priceless.

"Yes, Chloe, I thought you were done for the night?"

"Hey, Joss, yes, I am. But I wanted to ask you a favor," she says quickly, planting her hands on the chair on the other side of the desk.

I raise an eyebrow and lean forward on my desk. "You know I will do anything I can to help, if possible. What's going on?"

"I have a cousin, Karissa. Her boyfriend tossed her out on her ass and she doesn't have a place to stay. I was wondering, since you were just having interviews and we have the emergency suites for the girls who need help, if she can possibly work for her place here?"

Chloe pauses and takes a deep breath. "I can vouch for her. Although I haven't spoken to her in a few years, she is resilient…"

I raise my hand to stop her. "I respect that you can vouch for her. You know I will do what I can to help. She can stay here. But as for working here, you know there is an interview process as well as a full-blown STD panel. I would have to see what she would be able to bring to the club as a whole… but, how about I meet her, and I'll see what she can do?"

Her face brightens, and she skips around the desk and wraps her arms around me. "Thank you! You won't regret this! She's downstairs right now. Whenever you're ready." She skips out of the room and closes the door behind her. I smile, stand up, and check my makeup before heading downstairs. I walk down the staircase of the club, breathing in the sweet scent of arousal and sexual desperation—my favorite scent.

Looking around the room, I spot Chloe already back behind the bar, talking to what appeared to be a petite redhead —hair cropped short, her body curved with her backside poking out as she leans over the bar and throws her head back, laughing at whatever Chloe is saying to her. Her laugh floats through the bar to my position by the staircase, throaty, rich, deep. If sex were a laugh, this would be it. Interest piqued, I make my way to the bar, stopping briefly to talk to my security team to make sure things are moving smoothly.

As I approach the bar, the redhead, Karissa, turns around and our eyes meet. Her startling green eyes send heat throughout my body as I take in her delicate features and her chest tightly encased in a tank top that is barely tucked into her tight jeans. I immediately picture her in an alluring outfit, her soft green eyes making someone melt. I smile softly as I reach her. *I think I found my third girl. Maybe more.*

KARISSA

"Don't look now, Mar, but the boss lady is totally checking you out…" Chloe's eyes watch almost expectantly over my shoulder as she speaks, and her words pull sudden laughter from me.

A woman—this mythical "Boss Lady"—is checking me out? Oh please. My head tips back with a light giggle even as I sense a presence behind me. Turning, I feel all the air leave the room as my breath catches in my throat at the sight of the woman standing before me.

I blink slowly and my mouth goes dry. "Boss Lady" has a presence that fills the room. *Wow,* she is so fucking gorgeous. It hurts so much that I feel a pang in my chest where Daniel carved out my heart. I watch as her hips sway provocatively as she walks, an impressive hourglass figure cutting a path through the room. Silky black hair swishes around her shoulders as she moves and her eyes a bright violet—they must be contacts—look me up and down. At her perusal of me, my lip instinctively sinks between my teeth as a blush warms my cheeks.

"Little cousin, this is Boss Lady, also known as Josslyn. But you didn't hear that from me." Chloe's voice tunnels through my ears, but I don't so much as flinch until she nudges me. "Speak much, kid?" Chloe, chuckles.

"O-oh, I uh, I'm, th-thank you, ma'am, for the hospitality." I almost groan at my stutter. *Real smooth, Rissa*, I think to myself as I try again. "I, uh, my name's Karissa."

She smiles. "It is a pleasure to meet you, Karissa. No problem. I'm … happy to help." The way the words roll off her tongue, I have a feeling she could help me in many ways. Finding the ability to orgasm again is one of them.

I blush at the thought and clear my throat. "What exactly is this place, if you don't mind me asking?" My eyes take in the surrounding area, sparkling in awe. As I look around, I feel my body move closer to her all on its own, until I can feel her heat, the scent of pure seduction tickling my nose. I have to bite back a moan.

"One of the few places crafted by women for women." Her dark gaze slides back over my body, and goosebumps follow her gaze, as she laughs quietly, the sound smokey and sensual. "Where all your wildest fantasies can come true, Karissa."

My core clenches. Her tongue caresses my name as if she is tasting me. The purr makes my head spin as if I am on a roller coaster. I don't think… no I know for a fact, that I have never had a reaction this strong to *anyone*. It is as downright unsettling as much as it is welcome. Daniel hasn't broken me.

"My fantasy is for this night to hurry so we can get these

beauties out of here and I can go take a long hot soak in the bath." Chloe sighs longingly, her elbow reaching to nudge me again. A brow arches in that way of hers as she glances between Josslyn and me. "Why don't you go check the place out, Rissa? I'm sure the boss lady can spare a few minutes of her time to show the new kid around…"

Josslyn's own brow arches as a sudden fire blazes in her molten eyes, directly aimed at my too-mouthy cousin, who merely smiles cheekily with a shrug. Boss Lady clearly doesn't like being given orders, or even suggestions from the sound of it. Still, a slow smile curves her lips as she extends her elbow. "Well? Let's get you acquainted with Femme Fatale, shall we?"

I swear I am gonna kill Chloe. Gulping audibly, I tuck my hand into the curve of her arm and she leads me away from the bar. Her long legs stretch deliciously as she prowls through the various people, and I have a sudden flash of me kissing up those legs until I reach her sweet honey. I may not have been with a woman since Lacey, but for Josslyn, I would fumble until I get it right.

I shake my head of the cobwebs while I take in the lavishly decorated club, the walls a dark purple with gold-and-silver glitter catching the lights in a way where, as people dance, the entire room feels like a dark, sexual fairy tale. The room itself is massive but seeing as how the house is more so the size of a mini hotel, it makes sense. Hanging above the sunken dance floor are large gold cages; some with scantily clad women dancing sensually alone, others in pairs. The cages with the dancers have a soft stage light roving over their bodies. However, my eyes are drawn further to the part of the room where there are large, plush couches set between sunken, lavender room-like booths that have shimmery black curtains. While some curtains are closed, you can clearly see writhing bodies in the throes of unmistakable passion. I swallow thickly, feeling my pussy respond to the deep moans coming from that direction, despite the music filling the room. Others don't bother to close the thin curtain, choosing to forgo the illusion of privacy as they pleasure each other.

Josslyn doesn't speak as she walks through the club, smiling at the dancers, who look genuinely pleased to see her. Other than that, I feel her heavy gaze on me and I know she is choosing to watch my reactions as we make our way. Finally making our way out of the first room, we enter a long corridor with plush carpets that my shoes sink into it. As the door closes behind me, the sound of the music disappears and the only thing you can hear are the soft mewls of pleasure from the few people in the hallway, who are standing in front of large windows that I almost miss since they blend into the darkness. In fact, the only real light in the hallway is coming from the floors that have small LED lights lighting the path and the soft, barely there glow of whatever light is coming from the windows.

"We call this part of the club the 'Hallway of Pleasure.' I am sure you can see why. It's reserved for customers to have a place to, consensually, live out their desires," Josslyn says softly, her voice somehow there but not. It takes me a second to register that she has spoken.

As we walk, we stop briefly before each window, taking in the various sexual acts, positions, toys, and outfits. Holy fuck, the outfits. My breathing becomes shallow as I pause in front of a particular window that gives a full HD view of three women with ecstasy etched deeply into their faces. One woman, in particular, is fully naked while her face cradles between the thighs of the woman in front of her, her breasts on display with clamps. Ms. Clamps has the first woman's head firmly grasped as she weaves her hands into her dark blond hair. She thrusts her hips up almost savagely, her mouth parting in pleasure. Behind the naked blonde is a dark-haired, heavily chested woman, with a unique-looking strap-on behind the bent-over form of the naked blonde. Ms. Strap-on is gripping the blonde's ass firmly while she thrusts deeply, making her heavy chest bounce and jiggle with each movement.

I jump when Josslyn presses a button on the side of the window and passes me a set of headphones that I hadn't noticed. I avoid her gaze and take the headphones, placing them over my ears.

The moans come through the headphones and I gasp at the sounds of their almost frantic pleasure.

"You like this thick cock inside of you and that sweet, dripping pussy, bitch?" Ms. Strap-on almost growls out as she slaps the blonde's ass.

A muffled moan comes from the blonde who has her face encased by the thighs of Ms. Clamped Nipples.

She laughs in response, "Let her speak, Rebecca. I want to hear the bitch."

Rebecca sighs and pulls the blonde's head up. "Diana asked you a question, Jessica. Do you like this sweet pussy? You're lapping it up like you do. Such a good, sweet, little thing." Her voice is hoarse with desire as she coos, and I feel my panties become moist as I listen to Rebecca's dirty talk.

"I love it. You're so sweet, Mrs. Jillian," Jessica says breathlessly, while Diana continues to smack her ass and thrust inside of her. Knowing their names make the scene in front of me a lot more real, instead of the illusion of watching an online site.

Diana laughs. "I bet you didn't think that when we invited you out tonight you would be our little sex toy, huh, Jessica? But we knew. We knew the moment you started working at the office that you would be our little sex puppet. Those long skirts and baggy blazers did nothing to hide that tight little body and an ass this perfect." She slaps her ass repeatedly, leaving a mark and making Jessica moan almost drunkenly.

"Is this your first time being with a woman, let alone two,

you little whore?" Diana reaches between them and starts to rub Jessica's clit in circles.

While Jessica moans a "yes", Rebecca keeps one hand in her hair, while moving her other hand to plunge her fingers into her own pussy. She shoves her glistening fingers into Jessica's mouth. "Suck, you little clit tease."

Jessica greedily sucks Rebecca's fingers into her mouth and Rebecca laughs throatily. "That's right, you little slut. You can't get enough of my honey, can you? Those lips should always be wrapped around our clits, fingers, and nipples. Isn't that right, Diana?"

Diana grunts, eyes blown out with desire. "Absolutely. And to think this little prude tried to pretend she didn't want us at the office. But we noticed how your eyes followed us. All it took was a night out here for our little Jessica to come out of her shell. Now her face is covered in your cum. Do you want to taste yourself, sweet Jessica?"

Without waiting for a response, Diana pulls out of her and grabs her hair roughly, pulling her around until her ass faces Rebecca instead. "Put my dick in your mouth and taste yourself. Taste your thick cream." She feeds the strap-on into Jessica's mouth gently, and Jessica greedily licks up her own juices.

"Mmm, such a good girl. Do you see how you make this cock glisten? Do you want more?" Diana asks, pulling the strap-on out of her mouth.

"Yes, Mrs. Stone. Please fuck my mouth," she pants.

Diana chuckles before slamming into her mouth, making Jessica gag and moan, her eyes rolling to the back of her head in pleasure at being used. My mouth goes dry.

"Her pussy is dripping, Diana. Such a beautiful sight." Rebecca leans forward, pulling Jessica's cheeks apart before dipping her head to lick her from ass to clit. Jessica jumps as Rebecca closes her mouth around her clit, sucking hard. "Mmm, absolutely delicious." She smacks her lips before dipping her head again, making Jessica groan around the strap-on.

"That's enough, Rebecca. Our sweet assistant hasn't earned her reward yet. The little tease is going to work for it." She pulls out and Rebecca sighs, giving her slit one last lick.

"You're right but wait until you taste her. You're going to want to have more. Speaking of more, Jessica, don't just kneel there, turn the fuck around and get back to eating this sweet cunt you love so much, you little fucking bitch." Rebecca turns Jessica around, pulling her face down before closing her thighs over her head and tossing her head back. Diana pushes back inside her pussy with a moan.

"There is no fucking way this is her first time eating pussy. That tongue is positively sinful." She grinds out, gyrating her hips to the sexual beat of Diana's thrusts. I feel my clit pulse in time and clench my thighs.

Enraptured by the scene in front of me, I don't notice as Josslyn unbuckles my jeans to slide her hands into my panties, running her fingers through my soaked slit to work my clit before plugging inside of me. I don't notice, but I also don't stop her, her fingers masterfully working my pussy in a way that I never experienced. It doesn't matter that I just broke up with Daniel, or that I just met Josslyn, or that technically she would be my boss. All that matters right now is that I give into the pleasure that I have denied myself for too damn long. I moan softly, my body feeling electrified with desire.

"Thank God we have all night because I need that head between my thighs, and you need to try this strap-on. It's fucking unreal. It's fucking me and vibrating on my clit every time I push inside her sweet pussy. Ugh." She grunts and starts to move a little faster.

"Fuck… I need that. We can switch off in a little bit. I want to ride her face, too, drown our little fuck toy with my cum. Then when we're done using her, we'll taste that sweet pussy after we tie her ass to the bed. You'll like that, right, sweet Jessica? Being tied up and used how we see fit? It's going to be a late night for you. Tomorrow, when you come into the office, I expect you on your knees under my desk for breakfast and under Diana's desk for lunch. Do you understand me?" Rebecca moves her hips as Jessica moans a breathy "yes", never stopping.

Fuck, I pant at the control being wielded and I wonder what it would be like to be Rebecca and to be Jessica. To be the user and the used. My clit pulses as Josslyn increases her speed and I move my hips in time. Desperate.

"Fuck, yes, it's your sweet face I'm going to picture when my husband shoves his pencil dick inside of me. And every morning you're going to soothe this pussy with your tongue. Mmm, yes, such a good girl. Taste my fucking ass, you kinky little whore." Rebecca opens her legs wider while angling her hips higher and moving Jessica's head lower, never letting go of her hair. Jessica swirls her tongue with enthusiasm and Rebecca hisses, her eyes rolling back.

Fuck.

"That's right, now come back to this pussy. I'm about to cum. Diana, make Jessica's sweet pussy come for being such a good dirty whore for us," Rebecca says.

Diana huffs and increases her speed, while lowering her hand to pinch Jessica's clit. As they all scream and shake with pleasure, I bite my lip as I find my own release.

In a daze, I stand still as Josslyn does up my jeans for me, before taking my headset and placing it back on the wall. I turn away as the three women all switch positions and I see couples touching as they watch their own shows.

At a loss for words, I avoid Josslyn's gaze.

She tsks and pulls me closer, tipping my chin with one hand. "None of that, Karissa. Giving in to your sexual desires is good but owning up to them? That is where you earn power. I take it that's the first time you've seen something so... decadent?"

Her eyes keep mine pinned and I nod, my tongue still glued to the roof of my mouth. To be honest, it was the first time seeing anyone have sex in front of me ever, let alone three women. It was also my first time coming for anyone other than Lacey, years ago. With Daniel, I never got off. I handled it myself after he went to bed. I forgot how good it could be with someone who knows how to touch a woman. Hell, I forgot how good it could be when you're with someone you're actually sexually attracted to.

She steps back and I draw in a hasty breath while she turns around and starts to walk down the hallway, "Hmm, not to worry, Karissa. There is all the time in the world to finally come into yourself. This is Femme Fatale after all. A place to lay out all your desires and partake in them." She looks back with a smile and I give a hesitant smile back before following her, to continue the tour, a small part of me hoping the rest would be as amazing.

❖

KARISSA

While the rest of the tour was highly informative, Josslyn kept a respectful distance for the rest of the time even though the sexual tension was thick. After she showed me the rooms that were reserved for patrons versus customers, although she didn't explain that much, then her office, as well as the various suites that belonged to the other girls who lived here, she showed me to my room.

Although I am sure I would be able to get around with little error, it was hard to focus on the tour when with every place Josslyn showed me, I kept picturing her touching me in that particular room. I am both disappointed and relieved when we pause outside of the door that leads to my room.

"This will be your room." She stands in front of an ornate door in the wing of the house that has all of the girls' suites. The other wing houses her office as well as her own set of suites. "You can stay as long as you need, but you will be working for me. I'll make sure you have everything you need." Her eyes look me over again, and I can't help but fidget as I feel her gentle critique. "Since you have no clothing or toiletries, I'll see if I or any of the other girls have anything you can wear for tonight. You and I will go shopping tomorrow."

She stands between me and the room, her hand on the doorknob. The symbolism doesn't go over my head. Josslyn is what stands between me and a place to call home and security in the form of a job and sexual discovery.

I nod. "Thank you, but I do have a small savings. I can get a few things. You don't have to…"

I trail off as her eyebrow arches, the only warning I get before her body shifts and her hips nudge mine, pushing me against the wall behind me. Her hands trail along my arms to cage my head in. "Karissa, you're going to have to learn something about me. I don't ask, I tell. *You* don't question, you do. If you're a good girl, I reward. If you're a bad girl… well, let's not get to that. In short, I wasn't fucking asking you, Karissa. I was telling you. I don't give handouts, so don't think of it that way. I assure you, you'll pay me back. This is me taking care of a prospective new girl of mine—taking care of you."

My mouth once again goes dry and I nod. Her eyes flash briefly before she trails a hand along my throat, squeezing gently before stepping back slightly and reaching past me to open the door to my new room.

Our moment briefly forgotten, I almost trip over my jaw as

she sweeps open the door to the large room, tastefully decorated with neutral colors and equipped with its own en suite. It is more than I expected and definitely more than I deserve right now, when I have yet to earn my keep or even know what that will even look like. My eyes slightly bug out as I look around the room. I thank her, after I am able to get my mouth to work. Although, whether I am thanking her for the tour, the room, or the ridiculously insane orgasm she gave me, I'm not exactly sure.

An enigmatic smile crosses Josslyn's face and she wets her lips before responding. "Oh, sweetheart, don't thank me just yet. We've still got work to do on you, training to put you through..."

She taps a polished finger against her chin pensively before stepping into my space. "But I do think you will fit just fine within Femme Fatale. In fact..." Josslyn trails off as she captures my lips and sweeps her tongue into my mouth with a soft, barely there moan. My body melts and I feel like I am right back in the Pleasure Hallway. My desire is so intense.

"Yes, you'll fit in just fine. Be at my office at eleven." She steps back and sweeps out of the room without a backward glance. I take a deep breath as the door closes and my legs almost give out. I make my way to the bed and collapse with a huff, eyes fixed on the canopy above me.

I'm not going to lie... I think I would fit in just fine here, too.

"**A**nd she said she's taking you shopping? Lucky bitch!" Chloe giggles with a shake of her head. She had burst into my room a couple of hours ago with a change of clothes. After a quick shower and change, we sat in the middle of my bed with snacks, while she peppered me with questions.

"Yeah I, uh, I guess she is." I pick at the hem of the sweatshirt Chloe had let me borrow, with sleep shorts just as soft on my thighs. "I don't know what to do. What if I fuck up somehow? I can't go back home and I definitely can't go back to Daniel. I have savings but definitely not enough to restart my life. Ugh, I can't believe I let myself be warped into this pitiful person."

Chloe's fingers lace with mine, effectively pulling them from tugging at my hair, as she grins. "Hey, pitiful or not, you don't have to worry. I wouldn't let you fuck up. Not that you really can and from what you just told me, Boss Lady won't either. You had a sneak peek of the club. Everything that happens here is consensual and I know you liked what you saw. Imagine every night, giving or receiving that pleasure, to whichever patron you're matched to?" Her eyes take on a faraway look and she licks her lips.

After a few pointed questions, she explained that I would more than likely be coming on as one of the girls that works directly with a very elite group of women, like her. I would be matched depending on sexual preferences and have to undergo STD checks. Josslyn would train me as she sees fit. While to some, the idea may seem degrading or be a hard no... after what I witnessed in the hallway and my reaction to Josslyn, I saw it all as an opportunity to catch up on everything I have been holding myself back from. I don't want to hide anymore and I damn sure don't want to go back to a closet full of sexual dissatisfaction. No, I want the freedom that Femme Fatale is offering. I want a new Karissa and I am going to fucking get her, personal roadblocks be damned.

She smiles, shaking her head and hugs me tight. "This is only the beginning of a new chapter of your life. A chapter that will be full of self-discovery, a true family and bed-soaking orgasms." She winks and we laugh. "Love you, baby girl. Get some sleep."

That night was the first night in a long time that I slept peacefully. Sure, my dreams were full of Josslyn and a mysterious woman between us as we recreated the scene from the window, but my version of peace was taking on a new definition.

JOSSLYN

I BENT OVER MY DESK, ASS IN THE AIR, AS I CROOKED MY FINGER and had Adelaide crawl over to me from her seated position on the floor. I called her in for an early morning training session. Based on what I knew a few of the clients, I hoped to pair her with, would enjoy. Among other reasons of course... like memories of her skilled mouth that rivaled my recent encounter with sweet Karissa.

"That's it, Addy. Crawl over slowly, sway that luscious ass and lick your lips. When called from your perch, you need to make them believe that you've been out of your mind with need to pleasure them, to have their sweet cunts in your mouth," I instruct softly as she comes closer and ends in front of my knees. Lifting her gaze to mine, her vulnerability is like an aphrodisiac. Eventually, she will be confident enough in herself that she will have to feign being vulnerable. But for now, that sweet look makes me ache to command her, to fulfill that unique need she has that requires her to please her partner in any way she could. A true submissive is hard to find, but they are even harder to keep pure and happy. You have to truly toe the line between being a true Dominant who helps bolster their submissive's confidence while still giving them what they want and need both emotionally and physically.

"Good job, Addy, now you're going to run your hands up my legs and push my skirt up before you pause. You'll want to ask if they want you to please them. Once they say yes, you do not hesitate. Now, right now, you're going to taste me from ass to clit. You're going to show me just how much you've been waiting to taste me. Now, be a good girl and make me cum. At the end of training, I'll reward that sweet pussy."

Panting slightly, she follows my directions to the letter. Addy tugs me just a bit closer as she places kisses on my ass, running her hands up to separate my cheeks before running her tongue around my rim softly, lavishing it with attention. With a sigh of pleasure, I separate my legs further, my chest on the table as she continues her slow exploration before dipping her tongue inside of my pussy, moaning as she tastes me.

I clutch the sides of the desk as I look back briefly and take in the sight of her perfect shape kneeling behind me while her tongue and lips pleasure me.

"Good, sweet girl. Taste me. Show me who you belong to, who you crave to please. Make me cum Adelaide." Her soft moans coupled with her rising lust send a jolt of power through me and I respond in kind, sending a shot of lust directly through her body.

❖

ADELAIDE

Desire licks up my spine as I cater to my boss, her sweet scent feeling like a drug. Before making my way to her clit, I firmly grab her ass and focus a few more minutes on her tight rim, making her sigh with pleasure as she pushes back on my assault, bending further and further. I angle my head and lick her slick slit, savoring her swollen lips before I take her clit into my mouth, working it gently with my tongue, wanting to build her up into an explosion. People often misunderstand the intricacies of female pleasure. Even at the most heightened point of arousal, there shouldn't be excessive roughness. Unless, of course, that was what was verbalized. But unless your partner wants the sudden rush of pain and pleasure, starting slowly and building them up makes that orgasm much sweeter, letting you build up and make sure they were ready to go again after.

Encouraged by her moans, I reach and slide one finger inside of her, teasing while I suck firmly, my lips wrapped around her clit. She pushes back against me and her sweet scent assaults me on all levels. My desire rises sharply and my pussy pulsed in time with my licks. I breathe in sharply and moan at her taste, working two fingers inside of her now. My fingers bend slightly while I work her over.

"Make me cum, right now, Adelaide." Her silken voice wraps around me in a haze as I do what she asked and quicken my pace both with my mouth and my fingers. Her pussy clamps on my fingers with a vice-like grip as she reaches for my head and holds it in place while I suck her clit and simultaneously flick it with my tongue. I wouldn't have wanted to move any way but the show of dominance makes me wetter. She moans loudly while her orgasm breaks over her, her juices flowing like a dam, over my fingers.

"Yes, now clean me up with your tongue, and then get your

sweet ass on my desk. I think you earned it," she says gruffly, and I do just that.

❖

JOSSLYN

I take a second to collect myself before I sit on my chair and face Adelaide's perfect pussy. She lies back on my desk, her legs splayed wide. I lean forward, licking slowly up Adelaide's slit, savoring the way her body twitches at the slightest touch. I hum against her and observe as her back arches, pushing her chest into the air. I work my fingers into her pretty cunt and enjoy as her body writhes and twists in pleasure as I bring her to the edge and back off again. I chuckle as she begs me for more. I pull her hips closer, letting her plump ass hang off my desk, and suck her clit into my mouth, ready to taste her cream on my lips. There is a knock on my door.

I look at the time, *10:59*, and I smile. "Come in, Karissa." I look up as she walks into the office, in a pair of leggings and a shirt that reads *Femme Fatale*. She freezes when she sees Adelaide on my desk. I try to keep the grin off my face.

"Come on in and have a seat. I'm in the middle of a... meeting. We can leave soon."

She nods numbly as I promptly put my face back in between Adelaide's luscious thighs and suck her clit in between my lips, flicking it with the tip of my tongue and then alternating between long languorous kisses to her clit and fast licks. Her moans reach a peak before she screams out my name. A rush of power fills my veins from the orgasmic rush. Drawing out every shake from her, I stand up and pull her in for a deep kiss, letting her taste herself.

"Wash up and be ready for more training tonight," I whisper against her lips. She nods, her eyes still glazed over as she wobbles off my desk and gathers up her clothes. From the corner of my eye, I see Karissa writhing in her seat and I breathe in the scent of her arousal. Her desire thrums through my body, making me look forward to our little shopping session.

I lean on the edge of my desk and l nod as Adelaide walks out of the office and closes the door behind her. Karissa's eyes bounce back between my face and the desk, seemingly still in shock. I know she is picturing herself in that position as well.

"You look like you have questions. I will allow them," I say softly, pushing seduction into my tone and taking pleasure from the shivers that shoot up her spine.

"Is she your girlfriend?" she stammers out.

I steeple my fingers, leaning forward on my cum-soaked desk. "Would that bother you?"

Her eyes flash with interest. "I don't think so. Not as long as she knew…"

Her voice trails off and she blushes slightly. I chuckle, pushing myself up from my desk and walk around until I lean over her chair, bracing my hands on the arms, making her lean back.

My voice pitched low, I breathe in her arousal before answering. "As long as she knew what? That I touched you? Made you cum on my hand? Made you dream of you and I doing everything you saw in the Pleasure Hallway?"

Her eyes widen and I smile. "Oh yes, I know you relived everything in your dreams last night, my sweet Karissa. When it comes to sexual desires, hidden or otherwise, I know it all." My eyes glow and she gasps as I reach to run a hand down her face to cup her cheek.

"Adelaide is one of my newer hires, much like yourself. But also, much like yourself, I feel inexplicably drawn to her. Did you feel the same, just now?" I lean closer to whisper in her ear, her stuttering breath music to my ears. "Can you picture her between us while her tongue laps up your sweet cunt? While I fuck her from behind? Or do you picture you riding her face while your face is between my thighs? Do you smell her on me? Maybe you picture you tasting her, rewarding her for being such a good girl while I fuck you from behind, making you my little sex toy?"

Her pants turn into a soft moan and I pull back, a smirk on my face. My sweet Karissa wants to please as much as she wants to dominate. It's a good balance, and between her and Adelaide, I would have everything I want and crave. I would make sure I have it.

"Do you, uh…" she clears her throat, trying to refocus her eyes. "Do you fuck all the new girls?"

I smile. "I interview and train. I have to see if they're cut out for the business, although it doesn't happen often. This was my first interview process in years and before you ask, yes I have tasted your cousin on my lips as well." I turn to walk toward the door. "I've had her scream my name and fill my mouth with her sweet cum. I've had her head pressed between my thighs as I came from her quick tongue and soft lips wrapped around my clit. But that was business." I shrug lightly.

She gasps. I see the question burning in her eyes. "Ask what you really want to ask, Karissa. It will be your last question today."

"When is… uh… my training starting," she stutters out, her breathing growing quicker. I close my eyes briefly at the influx of desire, fueling my power. If I didn't know any better, I would say she was in orgasmic bliss from the thoughts alone.

"Oh, Karissa. Your training has already begun. The moment I touched you, I knew I would be keeping you… at Femme Fatale." I toss her a smirk and grab my coat, choosing to keep Adelaide's juices on my lips while we shop.

"Come now, Karissa, we have quite a few things to do before tonight."

Chapter Five

KARISSA

Four hours, a new haircut, a new low-cut revealing outfit, and an armful of bags later, I am still reeling from what I walked in on. Even more so, I want everything she offered and more. Despite my initial shock, watching Adelaide cum so hard from Josslyn's mouth soaked me immediately. But knowing that I am going to subjected to the same? I'm not sure how I managed to focus enough to shop, let alone spend time with Josslyn, casually chatting about expectations. Especially when every time I took a deep breath, I could smell Adelaide and it made me want more.

My mouth practically waters at the thought as I blow out a breath and set all my shopping bags down so we can grab a late lunch.

Josslyn chooses a small restaurant and we quickly order.

"Please, dear God, tell me we're almost done." If the pleading isn't already in my voice, I am certain it is in my eyes. My feet hurt and I'm tired of spending money, especially because that money isn't mine.

Josslyn's head tips back as she laughs lightly, her dark hair falling over her shoulders in waves and her eyes sparkling. God, she is gorgeous. "Yes, we're almost done. Just a few more things." Her dark eyes run along the length of my body, heating me from the inside out, as her tongue darts out to wet her lips. "I can't very well allow you to work in my club in sweats and a hoodie, even if they do have our logo on them. The outfit change and the haircut were a wonderful start, especially with a body and features like that. It's a crime, really, that you keep it covered up with self-doubt. I won't allow it anymore. So, next stop, lingerie."

My cheeks heat to an impossible color at her praise. I haven't even started working and I already think I can't handle it—handle her. But I want to, and I have had enough of giving in to the small voice in my head, telling me to settle for what I don't truly want. So, fuck that voice.

"Karissa." Josslyn's tone is gentle yet clipped as she snaps me out of my thoughts, her dark eyes boring into mine. "Focus. I understand this may be new to you but these clothes aren't just for you to *look* nice and dress for your position within Femme Fatale. They are *armor*. The right clothing has the ability to make you feel sexy, confident... powerful. And, my sweet Karissa, it is painfully obvious you have been powerless for a long time, if not your entire life. We are going to change that. However, you need to be present at all times. I don't play second fiddle, even to your thoughts. You'll be held to the same standard of excellence I demand from all my employees. Even more so. Now, get out of your head."

My breathing hitches, the intensity of her gaze combined with the conviction in her tone making my shoulders curl slightly. *No.* Shaking my head, I pull my shoulders back, mimicking her confidence.

Josslyn nods her head, a smirk quickly flitting across her face. "Good. Now eat."

I blink down, noticing the food in front of us. I didn't even realize they had delivered it, such was the power of being around Josslyn; everything else quickly faded into the background.

I tuck into my food, suddenly starving. After a few bites, I can't help noticing that Josslyn doesn't touch her food. Instead, she sips on wine, observing me. It's a comfortable sort of perusal, but I am still curious.

"Aren't you going to eat?" I ask.

She shrugs lightly. "I require a different sort of... meal. Not the sort that I can get from regular food."

I frown slightly. "What sort of meal?"

"In due time, Karissa," she responds, her tone shutting down that line of questioning. I nod.

Still curious, I take another bite of my food and try to think of another angle. Suddenly, remembering her dislike for too many "why" questions, I clear my throat. "May I ask you a few questions?"

She smiles briefly, looking at me over the rim of her wine glass and nods.

"Do all the employees live at the... club?"

"No. Our girls who work with patrons live in-house, myself, as well as my dedicated security team. You won't see them much. They tend to fade into the background. But I do have enough rooms to house if the dancers need to stay for any reason."

Then I ask the question that has been burning a hole in my brain. "How do you match the... patrons with the girls?"

She sets her glass down and leans forward slightly. "Each one of my girls have a certain... predilection and a talent that matches. For example, think of the Pleasure Hallway, what did you notice from those three women?"

I consider her words, trying to contain the flash of heat that accompanies that memory. "The two women, Rebecca and Diana, were controlling Jessica? But Jessica seemed to love it."

"Almost, but not quite." She hummed. "Control is an interesting concept, is it not? The ability to influence someone completely, to make them do anything you want, even be a pleasure puppet. The feeling of such power can be quite heady, fills you with a purpose. But often, it is simply an illusion because in that situation, they weren't *controlling* Jessica. Not exactly anyway. They were controlling the situation. As you mentioned, Jessica was enjoying herself. Tell me, what else did you notice?"

"They were very verbal." My voice wavers and I look away from her intense gaze that seems to pick up everything.

"Yes. They asked her if she was enjoying herself and made sure she responded to their questions. Despite being in the throes of passion, they cared that Jessica was consenting and still enjoying herself. Jessica, despite the intensity of the situation, still retained her power and everyone involved was on the same page. Same thing goes for the window. They could have closed the curtains for privacy but they consented to being viewed. Consent is the most important thing in any sexual relationship." She looks at me full on when she says that and I bite back the urge to groan and yell *I consent, take me.*

"Anyway," she leans back with a wave of her hand, "those two women were the Dominant partners in that situation and Jessica was what we would call a submissive. She enjoyed being under the control of her Doms and they enjoyed having a sub. Same thing for Femme Fatale. Some patrons like to dominate, others like to be dominated, and they are therefore matched to one of my girls that will either be submissive or Dominate. Some patrons like pain with their sexual experiences, so I have one girl in particular who specializes in drawing the line between pleasure and pain without crossing dangerous lines."

"Pain?" I ask, intrigued, although I know pain doesn't appeal to me sexually or otherwise.

"Whips, blood play with knives or other tools. All things that are made absolutely clear beforehand." She shrugs.

I soak it all in, enjoying her openness for the moment. "What if a Dom takes it too far?"

Her lips curl and her face turns to stone. A shiver of fear crawls up my spine as the room suddenly feels colder. "There is an unspoken responsibility that a true Dom will take on no matter who they have a relationship with. A submissive submits to their Dom with an understanding that their Dom will protect them and cherish them. It is a relationship based on mutual trust and respect. A Dom who hurts their submissive, physically, or emotionally is not a Dom at all. Even outside of a Dom/sub situation, anyone who crosses that line in my club, employee or patron, will not leave it alive."

I nod, at a loss for words, as her face quickly transforms from feral back to pleasant in the blink of an eye.

"Any other questions?"

I clear my throat, getting myself together. "Uh... what if you enjoy being submissive sometimes but also like to dominate?"

She laughs. "Some like variety, yes. But... are you asking me something, Karissa, or trying to tell me something?"

I find I much prefer her happiness rather than the intense anger from moments ago. Her smile takes my breath briefly, and I feel myself squirm, my thighs clenching. "I think I would enjoy something like we saw yesterday, but I think, under certain circumstances, I would be willing to let... someone... take control," I say it all in a rush, slightly embarrassed but pleased by my candor.

It doesn't take a genius to understand that my "someone" is

her. Her eyes briefly flash with desire and my core responds in kind.

A brow arches in challenge as she leans forward, legs uncrossing and spreading, her voice pitched low, enticing. "Oh, Karissa, you can certainly be my little plaything. I will play your body like an instrument until you can't see past your own desire. As for wanting to dominate, although being submissive is not in my nature, I can teach you how to play with your dominant side." She leans over so we are practically nose to nose, her breath purring against my lips. "And I know exactly who would be perfect for us."

A soft whimper breathes past my own lips as I slump away from her, trying to catch my breath and avoid embarrassing myself in this restaurant by begging for her to take me.

Her lips tilt into a smirk as she straightens, nodding dismissively at the food in front of me. "You should finish eating. You'll need all the strength and energy you can get."

That is all the encouragement I need to finish off my meal while trying my damndest to wonder just how much energy I'll be expending with her. Although to be honest, I couldn't care fucking less if I am drained dry. With her, it would be worth it. If she's able to give me such an intense orgasm just with her hand alone, I can just imagine being at her mercy, much like Adelaide was this morning. I want it. No, I need it. I crave it. I crave her.

KARISSA

Once we finish lunch, she leads me back through the mall to an expensive-looking boutique in the back corner. This part of the mall seems darker, edgier almost. All these shops seem to have one thing in common—sex. Whether it's lingerie, or toys, or massages with masseuses who no doubt did some things under the table, judging by the sounds echoing around. Did we enter an alternate universe? What the hell is this place?

"This, sweet Karissa, is my little slice of kinky paradise." She walks confidently, as if she's been here a billion times. A smirk tilts her lips as she pauses in the middle of the aisle, deciding where to go first. She turns to me, passes me a shopping basket and asks, "What kind of toys do you like?"

I sputter for the next several seconds as I follow her toward the sex toy section, surprised I don't burst into flames. She adds a variety of toys, dildos, nipple clamps and other stuff that I don't recognize. The basket in the crook of my arm is heavy, but Josslyn doesn't seem to care as she continues to add to it.

"Uh, no idea really. I've used vibrators for my clit mostly..." I finally answer, my voice trailing off as my face heats with embarrassment.

She clicks her tongue. "That won't do, Karissa. How can I expect you to please a client, another woman, if you don't know how to really pleasure yourself? Or..." her head dips as her eyes roam over my face.

"My ex didn't really like for me to use toys. Said they would stop him from being able to measure up to something mechanical."

She rolls her eyes in response. "A cry for help if I ever heard one. Toys enhance, not detract. His insecurities were no reflection of you, just of his inadequacies." Her breasts press against mine as she leans across me to grab a curved dildo, purring against my skin, "But don't worry, I'll teach you how to use them."

Before I can answer, I hear a familiar voice and my head snaps to the side. Daniel is in the corner, hugged up on a slim redhead, hands up her skirt, while she giggles at a display of riding crops and leather outfits. My eyes bug out and a soft gasp leaves my mouth before I can stop it. Josslyn turns her head and looks right at me.

"Know them?" she asks, her eyebrow raised.

"That's my boy... I mean, ex-boyfriend," I grate out, my jaw clenched. I had just left and here was the proof that he had, in fact, been cheating on me, with someone who looked just like me. I'm not sure if that is flattering or just wrong. If he is trying to appease himself, knowing he is a scumbag or if he just has a very particular type.

"Hmm." She purses her lips and a wicked grin crosses her face before disappearing. Turning away, she tugs my hand and striding with an air of confidence, she leads me over to a set of private dressing rooms, grabbing several outfits on the way. I ignore the shot of electricity that comes from her touch. A shot that goes straight to my lower regions.

"Karissa," she says loudly. "I think you would look absolutely divine spread out on my bed in this particular outfit." She grins mischievously and holds out a green-leather two-piece equipped with chains. The chains wrap around the small hooks on either side of the breast before leading to a skimpy leather panty that could be zipped right down the crotch. She holds it up to my body, her head turning to the side as she, presumably, pictures me in it. The green of the leather would complement my hair and certainly my green eyes. Despite my initial flash of reluctance, the way her eyes spark at the idea of me in this, makes me want it.

"Go put this on for me," she says with a slightly feral smile and I feel eyes on me.

"I'm not sure I can…" I start but trail off, my eyes flickering back and forth, hoping Daniel has left the store. Being close to him, especially in the presence of Josslyn, doesn't sit well with me. He is part of the old Karissa and I am embracing the new me. Shaking my head slightly, I let out a breathe, and steel myself. No, he doesn't get to ruin anything for me anymore.

"You can, and you will. Embrace your confidence, your power. No one gets to take that from you, so don't give it away. What's it gonna be, sweet little Karissa? Your power? Or your fear?" She stands tall, that damn brow arched, as she waits for my answer.

I nod, a hesitant smile turning into a full-fledged one. "My power."

"Good girl." She matches my smile before grabbing my shoulders and pushing me into the dressing room, following behind me.

"Now, this time, I will help you." Her voice changes, taking on a darker tone that sends shivers down my spine.

I turn to look at her. In what seems like a blur, she pushes me against the wall, bracing her arms up around my head as her hips push against mine.

"Consider *this* part of your training, Karissa." Her lips draw a pattern down my neck and I shudder out a breath.

"This?" I ask.

"The time for questions is over. I won't allow them. No matter where we are, you will submit to me. Especially when your body calls for me. I can fucking smell your arousal, little girl. Let yourself go. Give in to me."

I feel a jolt of lust as she looks into my eyes and my lips part as my tongue darts out to lick my lips. I feel my body lean toward her of its own volition and I nod, having lost my ability to speak.

"That's a good girl." Josslyn's voice is a quiet purr as she breathes against my neck, her fingers twining with mine as she pulls them up over my head. "Keep your hands there until I ask you to move them." Her hands trail down my arms and over my breasts. My nipples practically seize up at the contact, hardening against the meager slip of hoodie that separates our skin. The hoodie rises up along my skin as she lifts it above my head, trapping my wrists. "Devil be damned, Karissa, you're fucking gorgeous."

Her breath fans over my breasts as she kneels in front of me, dragging the sweats down to my ankles. The pulse picks up in my clit as I whimper, trying to close my legs tighter, even as much as I want to thrust my pussy in her face. My legs shake with the force of holding me still as my fingers lock together. She chuckles. "Mhm," she hums, air blowing directly on my clit. "So fucking responsive, sweet Karissa."

Just when I think I can't take anymore, she stands up, finishes undressing me, and all business once again, she moves to step out of the dressing room, pointing to the outfit on the hanger. "Put it on. I'll be outside."

I have no idea how she even moved or turned on and off so quickly, but her ability to keep me on edge turns me on and frustrates me. F*uck. *I want her to touch me, on top of me, inside me.*

I shake the thoughts from my head and close the curtain behind her, quickly stepping into the outfit. The straps, although unfamiliar, are not too difficult to figure out. After some adjusting, I look in the mirror and freeze at my reflection. Running my hands down my body, I never thought I would see myself dressed in something so provocative, so sexy, so… perfect.

"Karissa, are you done?" Josslyn pushes open the curtain and I turn to face her, forcing my hands to stay at my sides as she looks me up and down, her gaze darkening in appreciation.

"Absolutely beautiful," she murmurs and I swallow thickly as she steps back into the small but lush dressing room.

Coming up behind me, Josslyn moves my hair, exposing my neck as she presses her body against mine. I suddenly realize that the brief respite from her abrupt departure was simply a tool, a way to build anticipation. My body responds in appreciation, flushing with heat. I watch our reflection in the mirror as I feel her nose touch my neck while she breathes deeply. As her hands came around, cupping my breasts, I shudder out a breath. *Fuck.* Her touch suffuses my body with warmth and electricity as she lifts her head to meet my eyes through the mirror. Her hands move to dip lower and I wait with bated breath, hoping yet dreading the moment she will unzip me and find me soaked for her.

I hear a gasp of surprise and I turn my head to see Daniel's on the other side of the half-open curtain.

Lost in the moment, it takes a moment to register that Daniel and his date are standing there. In truth, I forgot he was even there at the store. Josslyn takes over every thought, such is her presence and her skill. Although, as I look back at the reflection, from the glint in Josslyn's eye, she must have known they were approaching. To be honest, I don't believe much of anything escaped her notice at all.

"Karissa, what... this... what..." Daniel stutters, his eyes wide, his chest moving rapidly as he sucks in deep breaths. Despite the dark edge of his voice, it is hard to miss the growing bulge in his jeans as he looks over. I bite back a laugh.

"Excuse me, I seem to have forgotten to close the curtain completely," Josslyn says, her tone not sorry in the least. In fact, it is tinged with laughter coupled with a deep smugness. A point emphasized by the fact that both her hands are still placed on my hips, ever so slowly moving lower, as if she can't stop herself. I find that I don't care. I want her to continue to touch me, to worship me, to make my body tremble as she wrings out every bit of pleasure she can. I don't care that we are being watched. In fact, it just adds to my arousal. Even if it is Daniel who is part of our audience, or maybe *because* he is... realizing that he was never able to make my skin flush like this, my pussy to drip with desire.

My heart suddenly feels full as I realize that Josslyn, with this moment, is allowing me to take back my power. I now understand a bit better what she meant about a Dom/sub relationship. I was choosing to submit to her, letting her guide me, provide for me emotionally and physically, and I relish in it.

"My sweet Karissa and I are just enjoying a private moment," She places a kiss on my neck before winking at me and looking back toward Daniel. She growls against my neck and the vibrations almost make my eyes roll back. "Isn't she absolutely fucking gorgeous? Forgive me for saying, but her pussy tastes like candy too. I just can't resist a taste, no matter where we are."

Before I can protest, she unzips the outfit and plunges two fingers inside of me, her thumb pressing against my clit. She swirls her thumb in circles over my swollen nub and I feel my legs tremble as I let out a low moan, my head falling back against her shoulder.

She looks at Daniel, then his date, before pausing to lick her lips. She winks at her, all the while working my pussy over, bringing me so close to the edge. His date sucks in a strangled gasp and Josslyn chuckles. "Looks like your date can use some of the same treatment. You're free to watch of course, for enjoyment... or to learn." She directs the last at Daniel.

"Sweet girl, look at our audience while I make you cum," Josslyn growls low, her voice a command.

I allow my eyes to meet Daniel's gaze as Josslyn curls her fingers while still rubbing my clit. She reaches her other hand to tug my nipple roughly and I come apart with a shout, the strength of my orgasm making my vision waver and my legs almost buckle.

Daniel clears his throat, his eyes flicking to his date, whose gaze is fixated on Josslyn's fingers as she wrings out every drop of pleasure from my body.

"That's right, my sweet girl. Just like always, drench my fingers. Mmm, do you see how responsive she is? She's so sensitive, and comes so quickly when I touch her, just like the good girl she is."

Taking her hand from my breast, she wraps an arm around my waist, keeping me steady as she takes her soaked fingers from my pussy and brings them to her mouth, sucking my juices off her fingers. She moans a low sound that sends shivers straight to my core. Although I just came, it makes me crave more.

Daniel's date lets out a low moan and I see her chest heaving, her face pink as she clenches her thighs.

Daniel stares at my body, transfixed, before his gaze falls to my thighs, soaked with my juices and he licks his lips. He shakes his head, catching himself as he snaps out of the spell Josslyn has woven.

Josslyn winks at Daniel, who turns around with a huff, grabbing his date's hand angrily, tugging her away as her head swivels to look back.

I laugh and Josslyn steps back, a smile on her face.

"I think he will regret everything he ever did now," Josslyn laughs. "Get dressed, I'll get a few things and meet you outside."

She leaves, closing the curtain behind her and I brace myself on the wall of the dressing room.

I take in my flushed skin, heavy-lidded eyes, and most importantly, the confident smile on my face. I like the way it looks.

JOSSLYN

I TOOK MORE PLEASURE IN OUR LITTLE ADVENTURE THAN I CARED to admit. The smell of her arousal, the way her body wept for me was a close second to helping her regain her power from her disgusting ex. Almost like fitting a key into a lock, I felt us sliding into a Dom/sub relationship. I was used to the sexual dynamics of my preferred predilections, sure, but I couldn't remember a time, nor did I want to remember, when I wanted to pursue something emotional as well as physical. It was uniquely refreshing.

Then there is Adelaide. There is something intriguing about her, a pure submissive, but her vulnerability calls to me in a different way. I know that together we will fulfill every aspect of our natures. I smile at the thought of both Karissa and Adelaide together. Yes, it certainly will be an adventure.

Usually, my level of power, my presence alone, would make even the most difficult of women give in to the pleasure they would otherwise deny themselves. But with these girls, I can sense that they want to give in to *me*. Not just the desire that piques from being in the vicinity of a succubus.

I smile as I walk through the floors of the quiet club, triple-checking the cleanliness of the rooms for our new patrons who are due to arrive tomorrow evening.

We have a waitlist that is a mile long, but with three new girls starting, I have invited those on the top of the list, to observe training and… sample… visually. As a favor to one of those on the waitlist for a long time, as well as one of the more prominent members of society, I made an exception, allowing her to bring someone she felt should benefit from the freedom Femme Fatale brought others. Typically I ignored requests but after hearing how miserable this young girl is in her marriage bed, Bethany, I believe her name is, I couldn't say no. After all, unhappily married women are my biggest sells.

Karissa is a long way off from being prepared, just coming into her own and learning how to embrace her desires. However that sweet, lack of experience can be extremely pleasing to some of those invited. On average, each girl will have a steady rotation of four patrons that are exclusive to only them. If the patrons wish to switch, I put them back on a waitlist. Which is why the selection and viewing process is very important. Who you chose becomes yours and you become theirs for the duration of their stay with Femme Fatale. Only a few of the girls have less than four patrons, and that is due to the intensity of some of the sexual preferences. On the side, they assist with training the new girls. Adelaide and Karissa are only going to be given two patrons. While they both have a job to do, that I won't take away, I would still be selfish, ensuring they both have time for me as well as each other.

A total of eight patrons are visiting, their tastes varying

from pain, whether it was giving or receiving, as well as giving or receiving pleasure. I sigh as I walk out of the patron hosting areas and walk at a brisk pace toward the training room where I have three girls waiting for me and two due to arrive to assist with the training. It is tiresome running a club of this size but the power from all the sexual activities has made me, easily, the most powerful succubus within the continent. While by nature, succubi focused on men, men hold no allure to me. Never did, in fact. I searched their dreams to find out about their spouses, those left sexually unfulfilled by weak thrusting and grunting. In truth, I found I had always preferred the company of women. So, it was to my benefit when I found that women were often miserable in their marriage bed. So the power jolt from turning a lifetime of sexual dissatisfaction into one full of pleasure was... incredible.

It was no wonder incubus, the males of our species were regarded as the strongest. The power from a female orgasm alone left me satiated for days. An entire compound filled with them? Well, let's just say no one has challenged my position in a millennium. It started off with a simple brothel hundreds of years ago. As years passed and times became more modern, it was easier to have specific clubs. Femme Fatale is the place where female politicians came, those tired of humdrum sex lives and wanting the pleasure only a woman can provide. And because women are stronger in spirit, my feeding of all the sexual pleasure has yet to drive anyone to the brink of insanity.

Walking into the training room, I take a look at the variety of plush seats and beds and ignored the three girls sitting nervously to the right of the door. I examine the toys, lubricants, whips, and chains. From the way the girls look at the walls and tables covered in varying sexual devices devised for borderline torture and sweet pleasure, I take note of who observed what, with varying levels of fear and excitement.

Adelaide, I can feel her excitement for the chains and the

strap-ons, loving the idea of being dominated. Jaime, her best friend, keeps drifting her attention to the whips, clearly interested in being the dominant. She will train with both of the girls who would be here shortly, as I do not sub for anyone. As I explained to Karissa, it isn't in my nature. Karissa kept her nervous gaze from looking at anything too long but I noticed the scent of her arousal seems forever present. Despite our early afternoon out, she is still new to her self-discovery, and her lack of experience screams throughout the room, making my appetite become ferocious.

There is a fine line between Sub/Dom relationships. While Karissa is slowly understanding what her role with me would be, my only hope is that she will quickly grasp the dynamics of how it will all come together with Adelaide. After our discussion, I realized a few benefits of the unverbalized proposal of a relationship between all three of us. I would have two very luscious submissives who would thrive emotionally and sexually under my care. Karissa would be able to explore her desire to be a proper Dom under my careful tutelage and finally, Adelaide would thrive with two true Doms who gave her what she needed sexually while still providing emotionally. As such, that is what today's session is aiming toward. I have a feeling Karissa won't disappoint, no matter how new she is.

I smile and slowly strip out of my clothing, their eyes rapt with appreciation as they take me in until I stand in nothing but my heels. I nod at the two girls who come in behind me. Caterina is a seasoned Dom and Trisha is a submissive who loves that sweet point between pleasure and pain.

"Good afternoon Trisha and Caterina. I want you to take Jaime here and show her how to be a proper Dom. I will take these two and train them myself." They nod in response as they lead Jaime to the side of the room with the necessary equipment. I turn my gaze onto Adelaide and Karissa. In a tone that brooks no argument, I say, "Both of you follow me into this side room. Adelaide, I want you on your knees. Karissa, on the bed, naked."

While Adelaide follows directions without hesitation, Karissa's eyes flash with a hint of indecision. Meeting my stern gaze, I feel the moment her desire flares. Biting her lip, she quickly follows Adelaide. *All in due time.*

JOSSLYN

Karissa lies on the bed, her hands covering her breasts while her legs gently open, exposing her freshly waxed pussy. I got the results of her earlier STD checks about an hour ago, which is why the training session is going ahead.

"Karissa," I purr as I take in her pale curvaceous form and flame-red hair on the black sheets of the king-sized bed. "Tell me, have you ever been tasted by a female before?"

"Yes... before," she breathes out, her voice light but laden with desire.

I hide the surprise and flash of jealousy of another woman touching what is mine before I did from my face. "That's good. The truth is, no one understands the female body like another female." I tsk as I walked closer to the bed.

"Adelaide, get on the bed on your back. Now," I command

and am pleased as she quickly gets up and lies down near Karissa. "I'm going to sit on your face and you're going to taste me until I cum all over your face over and over. Maybe then I'll reward you. Understand?" She nods excitedly.

Karissa's breathing becomes haggard, as she lets out a small moan, her chest moving irregularly as she watches me open my thighs and settle onto Adelaide's face. Her arms wrap around my thighs and settle me closer to her mouth as she takes a deep breath of my scent and shudders before wrapping her lips around my clit. I close my eyes briefly as she expertly suckles and licks me.

Without opening my eyes, I demand, "Karissa, come closer and open your legs for me."

❖

KARISSA

The air leaves my lungs in a gasp as I gape at her. The similarities between this moment and the one from the window make it hard to think. But I nod, slowly inching closer, enraptured by the sounds of licking, sucking, and pleasured moans coming from Adelaide. I gasp in surprise as Josslyn's hand grips my bicep and she pulls me closer. I land against Adelaide's side with a thump, but she barely flinches, too consumed with her task in Josslyn. My eyes meet Josslyn's through hooded lashes as I suck on my bottom lip.

"When I call you, you come over quickly. Now, spread your legs on either side of Adelaide's head, so I can eat that pretty little pussy." Her tone is dark and sensual, and a shiver breaks out across my skin. "Now."

I gnaw on my lip as I crawl over to where she wants me, closing my eyes briefly as I slowly slide my legs open for her.

The breath freezes in my lungs as she stares at my pussy. Her warm hands smooth along my thighs as she purrs softly against my skin. "Relax, sweet Karissa. You've already come for me before. Now I'm going to show you just how good you can feel. " She massages deeply into my muscles, soothing and relaxing me just like she said. Then, an equally warm wetness, her tongue, strokes the same thigh she's worked into mush with her hands.

"Jesus," I hiss, my fingers fisting the sheets beneath me as I jump.

"Oh, honey." She smirks. "I'm nowhere near your pussy. Just wait." Her tongue trails up my thigh, closer and closer to my pussy, as I breathe harshly through my nose and suck in air like a fish. "Mhm, you're already soaked, my dear sweet Karissa."

I don't doubt it.

I gasp sharply as she slaps my exposed pussy hard. "That is for not moving fast enough when I called you. Don't do it again," she growls softly. I pant, unable to respond but I soon lose my ability to think anyway as her tongue drags along my right lip, over my clit, and down my left lip. Before I can catch my breath, she flattens it against my center, pulling a shiver from my very depths as she sucks her mouth around my clit once again.

"Fuck!" My eyes almost roll as her lips press against my clit while her tongue flicks out gently. My hips eagerly rise to meet her mouth, as my hands instinctively drop down to bury in her hair, my legs locking around her shoulders. "Yes." The words stutter past my lips as I hold her tight against me, my hips gyrating against her face.

Josslyn reaches out to remove my hands from her hair and unlock my legs. I blink as I meet her dark gaze. "Mhm, I knew you'd be excited, but there will be no holding me in place. I determine your pleasure, not you. That is more for you and Adelaide. Don't make the mistake again." She yanks viciously on a nipple and I squeal as wetness floods between my legs. "You're so fucking responsive. That's such a good girl, sweet Karissa. Lie back and relax. Let me give you your first orgasm from a real woman's tongue."

Before she fulfills her promise, she leans up, grabbing Adelaide's head while she grinds down on her face, her eyes closing with a soft moan. "Yes, Addy. Fuck me with that skilled mouth. Ugh," she grunts as Adelaide moans, the sound of her licks increasing. "Squeeze your breasts for me, Karissa. Let me see your hands touch what belongs to me."

I do what she asks, my heart leaping with joy at her calling me hers, because I want to be.

She groans as she leans closer, sticking her tongue in my pussy before moving to suck my clit into her mouth. I resist the urge to move my hips as she pulls me closer, her hands gripping my ass firmly, pulling my cheeks apart as she dips her tongue to swirl around my asshole. I jolt in surprise at the intensity of pleasure as she enjoys my tight rim. Finally, she moves back to my clit. As her moans increase against me, her tongue and teeth urge me closer to orgasm until it slams through my body like a freight train.

Crawling down Adelaide's body, I watch as she kisses her deeply, her lips still soaked with my cum.

"Mmm, Karissa, you taste delightful when mixed with my juices and Adelaide's sweet mouth," she purrs.

She pulls away to lie in the middle of the bed, her hair splayed out, her hands running along the length of her body while Adelaide and I watch, as if under a spell.

"I want both of you girls between my legs. Now," she commands, opening her legs wide.

Adelaide and I look at each other briefly, our bodies tight with tension as we move closer. Our breath mingles and I follow her lead as we settle between Josslyn's legs, drawing our tongues up Josslyn's slit slowly.

"That's right, my sweet girls, taste me. I want to feel both of your mouths on me at the same time unless I say otherwise."

I bite back a moan as I run my hands up her thighs, placing one hand on her hip and the other I rest on Adelaide's free hand, tangling our fingers. Our eyes meet as we draw our tongues up to Josslyn's clit, softly teasing it. After a few seconds, we develop a rhythm, our tongues swirling up, down, and in small circles. Our tongues tangle and I resist the urge to stop to capture her lips with mine. She moves her face lower, to plunge her tongue into Josslyn's dripping pussy, allowing me to wrap my lips around her clit, to suck and tease. We switch and Adelaide sucks Josslyn's clit into her mouth, increasing her speed while I take Josslyn's honey into my mouth.

Josslyn's back arches and with a hiss, she comes. Wrapping her hands into our hair, she pulls us up slightly, pushing our faces together. Without a word, I feverishly claim Adelaide's lips with a moan. Our lips meet with a desperate clash and I lean up to grab her face, biting her lips and teasing her seam with my mouth. I barely register Josslyn letting our heads go as I breathlessly run my lips down Adelaide's neck, placing wet kisses, biting softly and then roughly as her moans increase. I place my hands on her heavy breasts, tugging on her nipples and she mimics my actions, before dropping one hand to plunge deep into my pussy, curling her fingers.

As good as it feels, it's not what I want. I want Adelaide between Josslyn and me as we take our pleasure from her and give her everything in return. Her body is at our mercy. I open my eyes and my gaze meets Josslyn's who is now kneeling behind Adelaide, with the same strap-on from the window. She nods once and I feel a thrill as I let instinct take over.

I grab Adelaide's hand roughly, tug her head back with the other and purr over her lips, "You're so fucking perfect, Adelaide, but you're going to be a good girl for us and get on your knees." Her eyes glaze over as she nods.

"How rough do you want this, Adelaide?" I ask softly, at odds with the way I sharply twist her nipples.

I can almost feel the weight of Josslyn's approving gaze at my question and I feel a spark of pride.

Adelaide moans deeply and her heavy-lidded gaze meets mine. "I… trust you."

I nod and move to capture her lips with mine before moving to bite her neck. I hesitate slightly. I know what I want but I'm not sure how to execute it properly. I look at Josslyn from over Adelaide's shoulder and she nods curtly. I know she will be there to guide me if needed.

I breathe deeply and pull her head down roughly to settle her head between my open legs.

❖

ADELAIDE

The thought of both Karissa and Josslyn taking control at the same time makes me feel almost frantic with desire. My body is overly sensitive, every nerve ending on fire as Karissa pulls my hair roughly until my face hovers over her pussy. I ache to please her, but I know better than to taste before being told. I shiver in anticipation, as I stare at her glistening pussy.

"Such a good girl, Adelaide," Josslyn coos softly, rubbing my ass as she nudges my knees closed, pushing on my lower back until my ass is propped in the air for her. I feel myself get wetter at her praise, and my core clenches in anticipation of feeling her slide inside of me, moaning as she savors my body and the pleasure she will take from it.

"You see how she waits for direction, Karissa? She could wait to taste you all day if you ask her. Such a good, good girl," Josslyn growls, before gripping my hips and sliding inside of me. I pant as she works me slowly.

"Grab my hips and eat my sweet pussy, Adelaide." Karissa grips my hair harder and the tugs drive me crazy with pleasure as I do what she asks, tugging her hips closer and burying my face to savor her.

"Fuck, yes, Adelaide," she moans, closing her thighs over either side of my head, muffling all sound. She puts both hands on my head, weaving her fingers into my hair to draw her nails across my scalp while she moves her hips gently. The touch of her nails makes my spine tingle and I moan into her pussy.

"You like the way I taste? Good, because you'll be there for a while. I'm craving your mouth, my good girl." Karissa moans as her hips move faster.

Josslyn slips her hand low, pinching my clit roughly. "You're our toy, Adelaide. Our own little fucking slut. Let me hear you scream into Karissa's pussy," she growls, slapping my ass sharply before thrusting almost savagely. I scream in pleasure, her words and her skill driving me wild with lust.

Each thrust pushes me further into Karissa, who opens her thighs to place her feet firmly on the bed to thrust her hips into my face. Every moan as they use me for their pleasure goes straight to my clit and I fight the urge to come.

As if reading my mind, Karissa pulls my face from her pussy. "You want to come, sweet girl? I don't think you've earned it yet. I think I want to see you on your back while I ride your face. Would you like that?" I nod as Josslyn pulls out, leaving me empty.

"Get on your fucking back, Adelaide. I want to see your sweet tits bounce as I throw your fucking legs over my shoulders and Karissa drowns you with her pussy," Josslyn barks, pushing me until I fall onto my back.

I lie on my back as Karissa settles over my face, facing Josslyn. She throws my legs over her shoulders, driving into me with a moan on her perfect lips.

I wrap my arms around Karissa's waist, sucking her clit into my mouth as my nose nudges into her pussy. She throws her head back with a shout and grabs my breasts, pinching my nipples. I let out a muffled moan.

"That's it. My two sweet girls in front of me, drenched. I think you've both earned your rewards. Adelaide, make Karissa come while you drench me with your cum." Josslyn picks up her pace, hitting the perfect spot and I increase my tempo, sucking and flicking Karissa's clit as I feel an orgasm building.

Karissa screams her release and I moan into her pussy. Josslyn works my orgasm out of my body as she groans out her own release.

After a few moments, Karissa climbs off my face to capture my lips with hers. She bites my lower lip before drawing it into her mouth to ease the sting. "Such a good, good girl. I look forward to having you be my little slut whenever I want. You'd like that, wouldn't you? Then I'll reward you by having your sweet juices on my tongue until you beg me to let you come. But I won't let you, not until you're shaking with the urge. I may belong to Josslyn, but you belong to us," she whispers against my lips while drawing small circles on my clit. I moan.

"Yes, I'd like that. I want it." My voice is barely a whisper as she works my clit faster. I toss my head back as she runs her lips down my neck until she reaches my breasts, biting down on each nipple.

"Then I think you've earned your reward. Keep those legs spread for me, gorgeous. I'm going to taste you," she says as she kneels in front of my pussy, her ass up in the air. Josslyn looks on with a smile before she grabs Karissa's sweet ass, lines up the strap-on, still glistening with my cream, and slams inside of her.

❖

JOSSLYN

Karissa screams into Adelaide's pussy as I start to fuck her savagely. She did so well for her first time that it drives me almost wild with lust. I couldn't resist her sweet pussy while it was on display for me, so while she rewards Adelaide for being our good girl, I would show her what dick, even if it is a strap-on, is supposed to feel like. Daniel is clearly a fucking joke, but with my years of experience, he will barely be thought as I work her pussy into submission.

I alternate slow deep thrusts with quick shallow thrusts, pushing her back so that her ass is up in the air and the angle is just right. She screams as I push deep inside of her, rotating my hips and flicking her clit with my thumb and forefinger at the same time.

"Holy shit," she breathes out against Adelaide's pussy.

"Don't stop rewarding our good girl, Karissa. Even while I make this pussy all mine, you still have a job to do," I say, my voice deep with lust and power as their desire feeds me.

I hear Karissa tell Adelaide not to come until she tells her to. The authority in her voice, while she commands her, sends a thrill of satisfaction, pride, and desire through me.

Adelaide's moans echo as Karissa savors her, her own moans vibrating against Adelaide's sweet pussy.

Smacking Karissa's ass repeatedly, I increase my thrusts before bending over her frame. I pinch her nipples before firmly grabbing her breasts. I push myself deep, using her sweet breasts as leverage while I move inside of her. She screams as this angle hits every nerve ending in her sensitive pussy. The strap-on sends shockwaves through my own pussy as it works me with every thrust, vibrating against my clit at the same time.

I moan as their moans increase and Karissa commands Adelaide to come. Karissa shouts as I rotate my hips, pushing her into Adelaide's who yells her release. Karissa continues to suck on Adelaide's clit as she whimpers in pleasure.

"Shut the fuck up and take your reward like a good fucking little girl," Karissa snarls before shoving her fingers inside of Adelaide, working her pussy while she laps up her soaked slit.

Adelaide's head moves side to side as she is overcome with sensation. Her back arches and her breasts are on display. I fuck Karissa harder, my lust reaching almost a fever pitch at the combined sight of Karissa's face in Adelaide's pussy, Adelaide's perfect form, and my hands full of Karissa's perfect breasts as I fuck her sweet pussy.

Despite all I have seen and done, I can't recall a single moment more perfect than this.

JOSSLYN

THE NEXT MORNING, MY HEELS CLICK AS I WALK INTO THE GIRLS' changing area in the boardroom section of the club. Every week different corporations hold their board meetings here instead of in a stuffy office, to discuss certain mergers and changes coming up. I'm not too keen on the details, however, having their meetings here gives everyone a certain advantage. My girls get to hear firsthand some of the most important things that are set to happen in our surrounding communities —some things that may or may not be advantageous to us. Then some of the most difficult of these many board women are more likely to acquiesce to certain requests when being given the best orgasm of their life, from under the table.

A bit unorthodox, but these meetings are one of the biggest money-makers Fatale has.

"Hello, ladies," I say silkily to the room, as I observe my girls dressing for their roles tonight. I observe as one of my girls gets Adelaide ready for her first real job of the night. Typically, I reserve the newer girls until after they are observed and chosen by their selective "owners" during the exploration show, but one of the chairwomen sent word that this particular merger is getting quite a bit of resistance from one of the major shareholders. That shareholder is going to experience firsthand the mouth Adelaide was gifted with. I ramp down the feeling of jealousy I feel, knowing she will be pleasing someone that isn't Karissa or me. Jealousy. I'm not used to the emotion and I damn sure don't like it. But between her and Karissa, I'm pressing some boundaries I haven't been familiar with in all my years.

"Hello, Ms. Josslyn," they chorused back.

I smile. "Before you take your positions under the table, Adelaide, make sure you are under chair number one and give it your all. As for the rest of you, you will take random spots. As usual, all these ladies are finishing up in the showers and will be fresh as daisies. After, you may all... reward," I pause with a smile, "yourselves as needed. Any pertinent information, keep in mind and we can debrief later. Have fun." I nod and walk out of the changing rooms and into the private booth behind the boardroom where I can observe what is happening. While I can also hear everything that is going on, the small details, the body language, and the hitch of a voice are better caught by the ones servicing the members. It's why their roles are so important. It's also why the girls could pleasure but could not pleasure themselves during. I need them to be focused. After the meeting, they could pleasure themselves, and reward themselves to take the edge off. Pleasing others is its own aphrodisiac.

I sot back on my plush chair, surrounded by an all-black decor with glittering gold lights and finishes throughout the room. I have one of the girls pull out an extra chair for Karissa as she is to arrive shortly to observe. Her reaction will be delicious to watch. I smile to myself as I reach for a glass of wine that was poured before my arrival. Tonight, Karissa will observe but I won't ease the ache she will have nor will she be able to touch herself after. Yesterday, she proved in many ways that she could be my sweet girl as well as a caring Dom. However, today is a new day and thus there is a new lesson. A lesson in deprivation. How will she react to Adelaide, after being left wanting, needing a release? More importantly, how well will she… resist… after my directive? Self-control is as important as consent, and being a caring dominant, you can't ensure either when you can't maintain control of your baser urges.

I hear the door softly click open and close as Karissa walks in, clad in a tight green dress that complements her eyes and I internally curse myself for changing her wardrobe to mostly form-fitting dresses. *Maybe I need a lesson in self-control myself,* I think wryly.

"Hello, Josslyn," her breathy voice whispers throughout the room and I nod as my eyes flick back to watch the rest of the girls take their positions under the table while they gently tease and laugh together. We may do sex work, but for all intents and purposes, we worked like a well-oiled machine. Everyone gives their all and works together for everyone's pleasure.

A few moments later, the corporation board on the docket for this evening settles around the table. The main shareholder, Mrs. Janet, sits at the head of the table, and what looks like her new assistant to the right of her, looking around a bit confused. But that telltale lick of lust touches her eyes. It looks like she may have just been briefed on what would be happening tonight and is struggling to contain her curiosity. The women are dressed professionally from the waist up and the towels that were draped around their chairs as they sat down are wrapped around their waists. They turn their attention to the main presenter, Ms. Vance. The PowerPoint flickers to life in front of each member of the board on tablets built into the table in front of them.

I feel Karissa's confusion and I deign to explain. "Every week, Fatale caters to various corporations built and maintained by women. They choose to hold their meetings here, away from the confines of their offices, as well as the confines of whatever marriages they may be in. Here, they discuss changes while receiving pleasure."

Karissa frowns as the presentation is underway and the girls got to work. I smile softly as Mrs. Janet's eyes widen and her lip drops in surprise before she skills her face and discreetly reaches under the table.

"Wouldn't that cause them to make unsound decisions?" Karissa asks.

I laugh. "Women are not weak. We are not ruled by our sex, but rather use sex to our advantage. While it may make the most difficult of people to be more willing to entertain certain changes, ultimately, women will still make the decision that will benefit the company as a whole. But there are some women... take Mrs. Janet for example." I pointed at her position from inside the room. "She tends to be more controlled, fearful of what her family will think with each change she makes. She's difficult to persuade for certain things because of that fear. The pleasure helps her relax and, after a few orgasms, she's willing to breathe and look at things more objectively instead of through the eyes of someone paralyzed by the weight of family nuances."

Karissa nods and her attention is riveted on the facial reactions of those sitting around the table in the other room. Soon, the power slowly starts to trickle through me, as lust pours through the vents.

❖

MRS. JANET

I reach beneath the table as Vance starts her presentation about a possible merger with another group. Her voice is perfectly in control as she is pleasured by one of the girls under the table. My core pulses as I wrap my hand around the hair of the one serving me today, someone I am certain has never worked with me before. Her expert manipulation of my clit as she sucks and gently kisses me at the same time burns through my veins. I hear every detail Vance is throwing at our group, as I lean back slightly and slowly pump my hips toward the eager tongue between my thighs, the girl's hands gently resting on my hips. I look briefly over to my new assistant, Bethany, and bite back a smile as her eyes glaze over in pleasure.

It took some practice but eventually, some of the best deals in our entire history happened right here in this room. Most of us are in loveless arranged marriages. Such is the life of the aristocrats, I suppose. But these meetings give us all a chance to feel the pleasure that has been denied us in the bedroom for years, the chance to be in control in other places other than the office. I crave the control that I receive under normal circumstances. Having to relinquish it to my husband, for him to demand my mouth on his shriveled dick is… distressing. Warmth suffuses my body as I hold this pleasure servant… closer. These amazing women are for us, to pleasure us, to taste us and that thrill is something tantamount to a drug. A delicious addiction that tantalizes my senses and has me curling my toes as this girl swirls her tongue from my clit and shoves it in my dripping cunt with no preamble. I suppress a shudder of pleasure.

These women don't know us. They don't quake in their

shoes when they walk into our offices or are asked a question. No, to them, we are people who just need the sweetest of pleasure they can offer. It is humbling and yet empowering. In just a few short hours, I'll be back here for the exploration meeting Joss is holding. After acquiring a few more girls, I am finally off the waitlist and will be picking my own Femme to visit every chance I can get. After tonight, I think I know just who I want. I tangle both my hands in her hair roughly and hold her close as she sucks my clit between her lips and laves it with attention. I close my eyes briefly as my first orgasm powerfully shudders throughout my body and she slows down, her sweet kisses building me back up again. I will break her and make her into my puppet. As she sucks my nub into her mouth, I suppress a moan. *Fuck, yes, I will definitely have her as mine.*

❖

BETHANY

I'm not sure how anyone can focus during this meeting. As everyone chats about the merger and its implications, my eyes glaze over as the girl below the table shoves two wet fingers into my dripping cunt while she sucks on my clit. I have heard rumors about clandestine board meetings but never any details. When Mrs. Vance told me I would be going and explained to me briefly the concept of pleasure relaxing the mind so one can make clear decisions that are usually held back due to too much self-doubt, I was in awe. Confused, a little hesitant, but in awe nonetheless. The concept has merit, but to know that these women, women I have striven to be like for years, used methods like these is mind boggling. It's no wonder they dominated the industry, making deals and changing lives at a better pace than their male counterparts.

I was told to listen intently and that is what I was trying to do. Part of me is engaged completely. I'm not sure how, but every word is stored in some part of my brain, while the other is urging this woman between my legs to fuck me with her mouth and make me come harder than I ever have before. Charles couldn't eat pussy to save his life, but like the dutiful daughter I was, I married into the family to please my father. Even if it means Charles breathing heavily on top of me twice a day, chasing his own pleasure in my curves as I counted to one hundred in my head. Not today, not right now.

It's like she knew exactly what I need as she curls her fingers inside of my pussy and makes me come harder than I ever have. My body suppresses a shudder and a shout of victory. I reach down to push her away and she briefly nips my fingers and holds my hands tightly at my side as she shoves her face deeper into my cunt and sucks and licks at my clit roughly. I look at the clock... forty-five minutes to go. I'm not sure if I will be able to walk after, let alone recount the meeting. As a picture of Charles flits through my head, I realize I don't care. I realize that whatever I do, I am also going to be in a position of power, a position where I can change the world. But first... another orgasm.

Chapter Ten

KARISSA

I BITE MY LIP AS I WATCH THROUGH THE ONE-WAY MIRROR AS THE women of Femme Fatale, take their time to pleasure these powerful women over and over.

The whole concept is as weird as it is genius, and I can't help but silently praise Josslyn. The concept is sound. She is able to provide a unique service that puts her business on the map. Not only does Femme Fatale cater to a small and elusive clientele, but it also provides a luxurious experience at the front of the house as well as a freeing one in all of the back-rooms. When you also threw in exclusive meetings where women can discuss business while being at the mercy of our skilled team… Femme Fatale is the best club anyone could have dreamed up.

My pussy clenches at the sight before me and unlike the

Pleasure Hallway, there is no sound. However, I imagine, from the look on the women's faces, that they are remaining on task despite what is happening under the table.

My eyes flick toward Josslyn, cool and calm as ever, not a flicker of emotion in her dark, violent, eyes. She watches the meeting even more intently than I do, but what exactly she is looking for, I don't know. Although, it does make sense that she would look after the girls in some capacity.

I close my eyes briefly, breathing deeply.

"Self-control is important in life but more specifically within Femme Fatale. Someone with poor self-control of their emotions, actions, urges are a threat to my club and my staff. I understand, more than most, that sexual desire often feels like an all-consuming fire. You can repress that desire until it's gone but more often than not, that repression turns into an inferno when it is finally released. It is in the midst of an inferno that the most destruction can occur, especially when in the middle of that inferno is someone not adequately prepared to help put out the fire." Josslyn's voice is smooth, quiet, yet filling the small space without her having to try.

I nod quietly in understanding. Do I want to be the person so desperate for gratification that I wouldn't respect boundaries? No. I also don't want to be the type of person that would seek pleasure from anywhere just to scratch an itch. I couldn't be Daniel and I wouldn't be Lacey. They are selfish with their desires and the need to fulfill *their* needs with no regard for my own. Fuck that and fuck them.

So I do what Josslyn does... I observe and I watch for any indication that the girls are being abused.

I am curious though. "May I ask a question?"

Her eyes don't leave the window but she nods and I continue, "The girls under the table with the patrons, are they not beholden to a contract?"

"I am the contract, dear. But no, beyond them working with

other patrons, there is nothing that says that they won't have to fulfill their other club duties. In their case, those duties are training related, these board meetings or for them to seek pleasure within themselves."

My eyes widen slightly. "You mean they also have sexual relationships? Like… us?"

She chuckles lightly before turning her gaze to mine with a lick of her lips. "My sweet Karissa, what you, Adelaide and I have shared and will continue to explore goes beyond simple sexual gratification. No, in situations like this for example." She waves toward the boardroom. "The girls would, naturally, get worked up. Due to the nature of the meetings, they can't pleasure themselves even with their fingers. So, after, I tell them to reward themselves in the dressing rooms. They take the edge off and feel refreshed. It doesn't turn into anything more. Although, if they were to want to pursue something serious, I wouldn't stand in the way of their happiness. In the end, despite it seeming unorthodox with everything we have discussed, we are a true family."

"Wow."

She smiles at my loss for words before turning away. Family is an interesting way to put it, but I guess there isn't another term for it really. Although I shrug internally, I don't think this is what Toretto had in mind in the *Fast and Furious* movies.

❖

JOSSLYN

I t's like forcing a jack-in-the-box back into its box. Karissa is finally given the green light to follow the path to self-discovery and embrace her passions, to then be told to hold back. It is necessary, but Karissa is like a sponge.

As much as she struggled with her desires at the beginning, I felt the moment she detached herself from them, focusing on the meeting as well as the answers to the questions she asked. I feel a trickle of pride.

At a very subtle nod from Vance, the board meeting wraps up. They are given a few more moments to enjoy the girls' ministrations before they are set to vacate the room. I stand up, feeling the power from the meeting flow through my veins. "Karissa, head to the changing room. You are to watch as the girls reward themselves for a job well done. No touching and no playing." I wait for a nod before I leave the room without a second glance. I need to prepare for tonight. Three new girls are a great thing. My issues with sharing Adelaide and Karissa are... not so great. However, learning to separate the business of pleasure from the pleasures that are being introduced because of that business, is going to be my own lesson to learn.

Chapter Eleven

CATERINA

I wipe my mouth and savor the taste of my client's sweet cream on my face. I understand the need to keep our hands from touching ourselves. I understand the need to prevent distraction. However, being a Dom has its challenges here. I need to be in control. Being on my knees in this particular part of the job is difficult, to say the least, but I make it work. In my mind, I'm controlling the orgasms. I'm controlling the movements. There is no pushing of my head. There is no touching. I touch you. I make you come and you sit there and take it like a good girl. I will please you, make you crave me, and make you realize that you need my touch as much as I crave your submission. It's why I nipped the hands of the girl who tried to push my head. That is a no-no. You're going to love what I give you.

From the corner of my eye, I saw the new girl, Addy, I think her name is, sweetly licking and sucking her client. I want her. Her submissive attitude pours from her, the way she fucks with her mouth while being held in place. Fuck. I want her and I am going to use the time Joss gave us after our session to claim her as my own. At least for now. I know Joss has already laid a claim on her. I'll be surprised if she lets anyone claim her in an official capacity tonight during the exhibition of new girls.

We all move off into the showers and changing rooms and I watch as Addy makes her way to the showers, her plump mocha ass swaying and bouncing with every step she takes. I make eye contact with the other girls, letting them know that I staked my claim for the morning. With their knowing smiles, I clear my throat as I stand behind Addy, following as she closes her shower stall. The stalls are big enough for four or five people with a warm bench that could double as a twin-size bed, soft warm floors, and rain-shower style showerheads. The wall has a small built-in closet with special strap-ons and soft leather whips. In short, it is a paradise for us. Josslyn treats us well and we are all very grateful.

"Hello, Addy, I don't believe we have formally met. I'm Caterina, one of the Doms of Fatale," my voice whispers across her neck as I press my hands on the side of the shower, caging her in. "This is the time when we are to take the edge off after taking care of the clients. I think you and I would be a perfect match to do that." I press my lips to her neck and take a sharp bite before easing the sting with my tongue.

She moans softly and I chuckle. "This is the part where you choose to give consent or not. Doms may get a bad rep but that's not how real Doms operate. So, are you willing?" I press my body against hers, her ass flush with my shaved pussy, her breasts pressing against the shower wall, her head falling back slightly, her perfectly plump lips opening in excitement.

"Yes, please," she breathes out and I smile. I am going to make her scream my name.

❖

ADELAIDE

When Caterina pressed her arms against the side of the shower wall, I felt my legs quiver in excitement. Although I want everything that was promised by Josslyn and Karissa, Josslyn made it clear that after the meeting, we could all play with each other. Since Karissa couldn't participate, I have no problem saying yes to Caterina. I want this, crave this—the temporary loss of control filling me with indescribable joy and the sexual gratification that follows. That is mind-blowing.

She grabs me firmly and turns me around, one hand wrapped in my hair as she pulls my head back and presses her lips up against mine. Her eyes open as her tongue tangles with mine, daring me to fight back. I moan as her other hand reaches down and grabs my ass firmly, then smacks it hard. My core pulses and my juices drench my thighs.

She runs her fingers through my pussy and shoves her fingers in my mouth. "Suck them clean, Addy, then get on your knees," she demands.

I quickly follow her directions as I watch her get settled on the wide bench, taking in her slim form and her sharp Asian features. Her long black hair falls down to her waist, her plump breasts high on her chest, and her tattoos down her side to the slight flare of her hips. I lick my lips in anticipation. I crawl closer to her on her command and breathe in her unique scent from her waxed pussy.

"You're so beautiful, Addy. Do you know that? Your chocolate skin, your lips, your hourglass shape. Fuck, I'm going to savor this. I know Josslyn has you as hers, but right now, I'm going to make you scream my name," she whispers as she wraps her hands around my hair and brings me closer to her core.

"Now taste me. Soon it will be me savoring you," she says as my tongue licks her from anus to clit, stopping to suckle lightly at her swollen nub. I press my thick lips against her clit as I let my tongue dip and explore, softly teasing her slowly to make sure her orgasm is as intense as possible. This I can do… I can please. I can make someone lose their mind. I love to please. I love to bring my partners to the edge and I love being cherished and cared for as a sub. I was once with someone who thought they were a Dom, but they took pleasure in breaking me down and making me feel worthless. It took a while to get back to myself. Jaime helped me by showing me what a true Dom is and I am grateful for it.

"Fuck, yes. Just like that," she whispers and I give it my all, my pussy clenching in response.

❖

CATERINA

Her mouth is a haven. Her tongue is decadent. I grab her hands firmly and bring them to my chest, using her fingers to play with my nipples while I tighten my thighs around her head, holding her in place as her tongue dips into my pussy and tongue fucks me. When she makes her way back up to my clit and suckles, I come so hard I see stars.

"Fuck, yes," I grunt as I move my hands to her head and grind my pussy onto her tongue. Damn, this I need more of and I am nowhere near done.

"Kneel on the bench right the fuck now. Let me see that pink pussy in the air," I grind out, reaching into the cubby to attach our specially-made strap-on that goes inside of me and vibrates on my clit every time I thrust into someone. I affix a thick dildo to the front and then run my hands all over her wet body, savoring the feel of skin and admiring her ink. Grabbing her plump tits for leverage, I angle my hips and slam "my dick" into her sopping wet pussy. Her deep guttural moan sends a sensation of pure fire down my belly. I rake my nails slightly down her back, pumping into her faster as her moans reach a peak.

"Reach down and rub your clit for me, gorgeous," I manage to get out, before I come from the double sensation of the dildo and vibrator. She shakes from the force of her orgasm before she collapses on the bench. She draws a deep breath and turns around, her breasts heaving, her lips swollen from biting them.

"Come here and taste yourself," I demand, wanting to see her lips wrapped around the dildo. I grab her head and push her mouth on my fake dick, watching her lick the sides and moan at the taste of her pussy.

"That's a good girl." I roughly grab her head, bend over and kiss her deeply. "You taste delicious, Adelaide. I'm going to need more of that sweetness." I unhook and set the harness to the side. She is so damn beautiful, her curly hair and her exotic features filling me with a frenzy I haven't felt since Josslyn trained me a couple of years ago. I want… no, I need to taste her. That kiss isn't nearly enough.

"Lean back and open those thick thighs for me, Addy. I'm going to taste you now until you come over and over, and then I'm going to ride that pretty face until I'm satisfied," I murmur softly, settling down on the bench and placing my face between her thighs. I run my tongue down her smooth pussy, moaning at the sweet taste. The contrast of her pink pussy, swollen nub, and her chocolate thighs shoot lust through me as I lap her up, drawing my hands up and down her body, savoring her curves. I suck her clit into my mouth as I reach up and pinch her nipples. Her moans echo throughout the stall. Unable to stop myself, I draw her hips sharply closer to me and suck, tease and taste until she comes over and over again, partially sobbing as I lay delicate kisses on her pussy, dipping my tongue into her one last time, savoring her taste.

"Such a good girl," I croon, crawling up her body, her face flush, lips parted as I thrust my tongue into her mouth, wrapping my hands around her throat, squeezing lightly.

"Now I'm going to ride this gorgeous face," I moan in her ear, sucking her earlobe into my mouth. Her breath hitches and I smile as I slide up her body and sit on her waiting tongue, grabbing her curls roughly as I take what I want.

❖

KARISSA

It isn't truly until I get into the changing room that I realize what Josslyn meant by having me watch and not participate. The girls pair up, even triple up as they start to work off what is clearly a lot of pent-up sexual desire. The lust in the room is enough to make my hair stand on end. Watching as these gorgeous women lick each other up and strap on toys to bring themselves to a peak is making me ache with pent-up desire.

Watching them in the boardroom was bad enough but this? The changing room is built for much more than its namesake. Each of the deep velvet leather benches, that upon opening make a twin bed, and the heated, red, soft padded floor where some of the girls are kneeling while either offering up their pussies or their tongues to the girls behind or in front of them —or both—are made for impromptu pleasure sessions. There is soft melodic afrobeat music coming from the speakers in the ceiling which seem to set the pace of how the girls are pleasing one another. The walls match the floor and toward the back are dark velvet and black shower stalls where I see Adelaide and a beautiful Asian woman head off.

I feel a dark hint of rage as I watch them walk away and I

struggle to catch myself from following and grabbing Adelaide. The wave of possessiveness takes my breath away and I am shocked at how quickly I find myself attached to Adelaide. I am surprised Addy is allowed to participate in an "after session" session, but then nothing should surprise me about Josslyn. Jealousy swirls low in my belly as I reflect on our time together. I know for a fact that other than club business, I don't want anyone else touching Adelaide other than Josslyn and me.

Silently, I follow close behind and stand outside the shower stall while Adelaide has her head between the legs of a petite, gorgeous, Asian woman, making her cum. I know what her mouth feels like, what her pussy tastes like and *it is mine*. A glutton for punishment, I watch as Addy's perfect pink pussy is on display before the woman starts to fuck her from behind, roughly. I stand there the entire time while they take pleasure from each other's bodies.

Briefly, it crosses my mind that *this* is the ultimate test of Josslyn's lesson about self-control. I have no doubt she is aware that Adelaide would have someone seek her out to find pleasure. I also know, without a doubt, that had Josslyn told her to say no, she would have. But Josslyn doesn't set any rules for this. In fact, since I'm not allowed to participate and can only watch, she has to have known I would see Adelaide in a situation. I sigh quietly and take a deep breath to curtail my floundering emotions. We haven't made anything official yet and it isn't fair to expect her not to want to release some pressure after being in that boardroom. She has the right to her own decisions.

However, I plan to show our sweet Adelaide just how out of control I feel right at that moment, in the sweetest of ways.

KARISSA

"The Exhibition is tonight. Are you ready?" Chloe asks as I make my way into my new bedroom. I jump, not expecting to see her in there, lounging comfortably on my bed. I roll my eyes. "Don't you have your own room?"

She shrugs. "Sure, but I like your bed better."

Ignoring her, I consider her question. "I mean, Joss has mentioned it briefly but I have heard the girls talk about it more in passing. I'm not exactly sure what I'm supposed to do."

"I'm sure Josslyn will brief you guys before you start. Me, I was naked, covered in glitter and we danced a little bit to the music. As to what you are supposed to do, you won't be doing much until your benefactor chooses you. Pretty much, you're going to stand behind a glass panel and you will be asked questions. Some may ask you to do a few things for the show.

Depending on how they rank your answers and your performance, Joss will choose who you go to. It also varies with the type of sex they prefer."

I sigh. "Yeah, Josslyn did mention that. Doms for subs and vice versa as well as those who want extreme forms of pleasure. The dancing I can do. I'm not even creeped out by the watching. I wonder what my patron will be like or if I will even like them."

I toss myself down on my bed and turn my head to stare at Chloe while she thoughtfully considers her answer.

"Josslyn has a weird sixth sense about those things. Also, she's huge on consent and contracts. Ultimately, Femme Fatale is all about sexual exploration and pleasure, not abuse. So if you hate who you end up with, she will never force you to stay."

I let out a breath, my body tingling with both excitement and apprehension. I'm not exactly sure what I have gotten myself into at this point but the idea of exploring that side of me that I have been suppressing, or avoiding, all these years is intriguing. But I know I would prefer to do all of that with Adelaide and Josslyn. In the end, I understand my job and I just hope I am paired up with an amazing patron.

"Okay, so Josslyn chooses one person and we work for them only?" I ask.

Chloe laughs. "No, girl. You'll be doing nothing most days if you only have one customer. No, typically you are given four patrons. They all like different things and eventually, you'll build up a pretty good relationship with them. No one else beyond that and if they want to switch down the road, they can. Or you for that matter if you ask Josslyn."

Biting my lower lip, I consider my position. This means I will probably see less of Josslyn and Adelaide than I want but it also means that every time I am with them, I will be more confident with my sexuality and pick up a few more tricks.

Suddenly, I am filled with purpose. I don't know how far things will go with them and I'm not stupid enough to think I will ever be with them exclusively. There are still pieces of training and business but I am done with not going after what I really want. I am going to be the perfect Femme Fatale and eventually, I am going to be the perfect combination of sub/Dom for Josslyn and Adelaide.

❖

JOSSLYN

I sit back in our plush exhibition room, while some of my girls hand out flutes of champagne. I let the lust build around me as I make the waiting clients squirm with excitement. Mrs. Janet is dressed out of her usual business suit and is dressed in a revealing burgundy dress that highlights her dark skin tone and pronounced curves. She has already expressed interest in whoever pleasured her in the boardroom, and after knowing her for several years, I reluctantly agree that Adelaide may work with her, as part of her rotation. Typically, these decisions are made after the entire evening. However, knowing her as well as I do, giving Adelaide to her as a client isn't too much of a hardship, considering I will also make sure Karissa is in the room with them.

She brought her assistant, Bethany, with her. She looked confused but excited to be here. From what I understand, Bethany is like most women I have met in my life and is miserable in her marriage bed. Her husband never pleasures her, out more for himself within his arranged marriage. Looking her over, I can see he definitely got the better end of the deal. Long brown tresses curve around her face and a short dress flatter her figure. What I love about her is the innocence that comes pouring off her in waves. Her body's plush with extra padding, just enough to hold for a good time bent over my desk. Being brought to the top of the waitlist is not a privilege anyone could say they ever have, but I have a feeling Bethany is going to be more than just a client. She will be a project of the highest order for whomever I set up with her.

I look over at Mrs. Vance, a longtime boardroom user, comfortably sitting back in her chair, observing the room. More of a submissive in nature, she wears a tailored pants suit, and light makeup, trying to give herself more of an illusion of power than actually having it sexually. Not everyone who dominates a company matches that energy sexually. She is pretty enough, slim figure and kind. Overall, I hope this experience brings her more sexual confidence.

Finally, Myia Day, a beautiful black woman with short curly hair, a slim figure with perfect curves, sits to my right, in a short black dress with a low plunging neckline. The tightness of the dress reveals her nipple rings and the fact that she wears no undergarments. Her Native American features cut an impressive image. I admit the very brief itch I have to enter her dreams and take her for myself is strong. But that is the curse of the Succubai, never satisfied and always needing, wanting more. Although admittedly, that voracious part of myself has seemed too quiet, I won't delve too far into that.

The lights dim and I hear the sharp intake of breath as Karissa, Jaime and Adelaide walk into the other room, on the other side of the glass, wearing nothing but shimmer body spray, makeup, and confidence. Despite seeing their moments before to brief them on what is expected of them, I bite back a groan as I take in Karissa and Adelaide's figures side by side, contrasting their skin next to one another. The way I feel my hunger both calm and rear up makes me certain that I will take both of them for my own. Eventually. No doubt about it.

As instructed, they turn around in a slow circle, bend over, and then sway seductively to the slow music playing on their side of the glass.

"May we ask questions and ask them to perform now?" Mrs. Janet asks as she leans back in her chair, crossing and uncrossing her legs as the sexual desire ramps up in the room.

"Absolutely. Although they may not be able to see you through the glass, they can hear clearly. Just touch the mic button on the side of your chairs. The pencil and paper are also on the side if you wish to write down your desires. These three are our newest girls. However, you can all write down your preferences for up to four of our girls and I will choose those myself." I nod. There are only a few girls with less than four clients and since they are all busy with current clients, I will help make the final decisions. They all have a choice in the end, but they rarely went against my suggestions, trusting my judgment and experience. Exhibitions are usually for the newer girls joining Femme Fatale. At any other time, the clients would peruse a book of profiles and photos.

The mic comes to life as Mrs. Janet's voice comes across the room. "Would any one of you consider yourself a novice when it comes to pleasuring a woman?"

Karissa nods while Jaime and Adelaide shake their heads. Mrs. Janet smiles. "To the ones who nodded, what might your name be?" Karissa sweetly, albeit a bit hesitantly, answers and her sultry voice makes my clit jump in excitement. I enjoy her lack of genuine experience. It provides me with the chance to train her to my liking, to have her panting with a need for something only I can give her—a pleasure so intense that it goes beyond the powers of my inner demon. But right now, broadening her horizons is useful to the club and to me... possibly.

Keeping my face blank I return my focus on reading the room. I send a wave of lust into everyone in the two rooms.

They visually shudder and shift in their seats, clenching their thighs.

Mrs. Janet's question isn't surprising. She knows everything she needs to know from the provided profiles, but she takes pleasure in having anyone admit that they lack a certain level of experience. It drives her sexually to teach and take control.

"Okay, girls, I want you to get on your knees, ass facing us, and touch yourselves." My voice penetrates the room and while the girls comply, you can see their juices glisten on their thighs, their bodies reacting to my power. Though not directly in front of us, you can clearly see their eyes blown out, desire making their bodies flush with color.

After a few more moments and a flurry of writing, each of the women hands me a sheet of paper with their sexual preferences, their choices, and their preferred schedule throughout the week. Nodding my head, I press a button on the side of my chair, and Karissa, Jaime, and Adelaide file out of their side of the glass.

As the new clients make their way out of the exhibition room to enjoy the club and the bar, I make my way to my office to work out schedules, sending word for the three girls to make their way to my office. Typically, I give forty-eight hours for anyone to make changes but as it is, all the new clients offered to increase their membership costs to start coming tomorrow. While all my girls typically have breaks throughout the week, tonight is my last opportunity to indulge in Adelaide and Karissa all to myself. Jaime, well, despite our similar predilections, I need her for my own visually selfish reasons. Tonight isn't a night of training. It is a night to see just how far this obsession for Karissa and Adelaide has gone, and if there is a way back. I have a feeling I already know the answer.

JOSSLYN

A soft knock on my door alerts me to their arrival if the scent of their distinctive lust wouldn't have alerted me beforehand.

"Come in, ladies, and lock the door behind you," I say softly, holding my hand up, to keep them quiet while I finish getting all the schedules wrapped up. Slowly, I let lust fill the room, while I put my laptop to the side and stand up from my chair.

I take them all in—make-up flawless, their skin shimmering beneath their robes. I frown. "Unless I say otherwise, you are to be disrobed when I summon you into my office, is that clear?"

They quickly nod, dropping their robes and I smile softly. Approaching them, I start to slowly disrobe, unzipping my dress and letting it fall to the carpeted floor, displaying my bare pussy and breasts. Their sharp intake of breath is music to my ears. My hips sway provocatively as I run my fingers through my hair and down my body, and I finally stand before them. Their chests heave, their eyes riveted to my body. Their greedy eyes follow my every movement, a silent agreement that they can look but not touch until I tell them to.

Reaching down, I open my legs slightly and caress my clitoris briefly while I make my way to my slick pussy and enter two fingers inside of me. Moaning softly, I pump a few times before I withdraw my soaking hand and shift to Adelaide. I press my fingers to her waiting mouth, her pouty lips sucking my fingers deeply, her greedy tongue cleaning them off. She moans and shudders visibly. I withdraw my fingers from her mouth and grab her perfect ass, bringing her closer to me as I plunge my tongue into her mouth, tasting myself on her lips. We moan, our hands roaming almost feverishly.

I pull away and push her toward the bed in my office. "Get on the bed, Adelaide, and bend over. I want to see your ass in the air." I look back at the other two while Adelaide follows my directives. "Karissa, lie down on the bed in front of Adelaide. Jaime, I want you to strap on and fuck Adelaide's sweet pussy until she can't think anymore."

Jaime barely suppresses a shudder as her eyes look almost blown out with lust. While she goes to my wall full of sex toys, I turn around and walk over to the bed where Karissa is laid out, almost shyly, her red hair lay around her like a halo. Simply beautiful.

I tsk. "Karissa, open your legs. Adelaide is going to savor that pussy until you can't see straight." My voice is firm, brooking no argument. Karissa opens her creamy thighs before Adelaide who immediately lowers onto her elbows, reaching through Karissa's bent knees, grabbing her waist, and pulling her closer. She effectively locks her in place before she lowers her head and presses a long, open-mouthed kiss on Karissa's clit, drawing out a deep moan of pleasure from her. I feel Jaime behind me and I hold my hand up, stopping her.

I walk up to Adelaide's bent form, her glistening pussy on display, aching to be touched. "Jaime, I want you to fuck Adelaide but before you do…" I lean over, burying my face in Adelaide's sweet mound, tugging her clit into my mouth right before I send a pulse of lust directly to her, making her gush with an orgasm, her scream muffled by Karissa's thighs. Karissa tosses her head, the vibrations from Adelaide stirring her into a frenzy.

I pull back with a grin aimed at Jaime. "Mmm, just needed a taste before I watch you fuck her senseless." I wave my hand toward Adelaide and Jaime wastes no time before plunging herself inside of her, moaning with pleasure as the strap-on simultaneously pleasures her as well. I walk backward until I reach the plush chair situated right next to the bed and I settle comfortably, my face still wet with Adelaide's juices, to watch the girls play.

Karissa's moans increase as Jaime's thrusts push Adelaide's face into her pussy over and over again. Adelaide's muffled sounds heighten the pleasure in the room. I watch as Jaime grabs the waist in front of her with one hand while reaching to slowly rub Adelaide's clit.

After a few seconds, Jaimie pulls her hands back and smirks. "You're not going to come yet, bitch. Not until I get mine." She smacks Adelaide's ass, hard, making it jiggle before she slows her thrusts and leans her body close, running her hands over Adelaide's back, reaching over to anchor herself with Adelaide's generous breasts before she starts to thrust inside her with hard, slow, full strokes. Burying the strap-on inside of Adelaide's greedy pussy, Jaime moans and her eyes roll to the back of her head. She's at the perfect angle to stimulate Adelaide's G-spot as well as create increased friction to the internal portion of Jaime's strap-on, eliciting a mind-blowing orgasm for both parties. Just like I designed it.

Jaimie screams as she comes, Adelaide following suit. The rush of power is absolutely delicious but the look on Karissa's face, her body flush with desire and her orgasm, is even more delectable.

But the show, although pleasing to watch, proves to me that, if it wasn't for business, seeing anyone engage in the sweetness that is Adelaide and Karissa is… infuriating. I have my own challenges with self-control. I am a demon after all, but it has been a long time since I felt a true inkling of the rage that I am capable of. In this case, though it is due to no fault of her own, the trickle is enough that I know I have to get Jaime out of my sight immediately.

"Thank you, Jaime, for the most delightful show. You are dismissed." Keeping my voice polite, I wave Jaime toward the door, her eyes still glazed over from her orgasm.

As Jaime quickly grabs a robe and leaves the room with a smile, I approach Adelaide, her face still in Karissa's pussy, making her whimper. "Adelaide, you may stop. I need to taste you on my tongue. Karissa, you are to watch while I please Adelaide. You are not to touch yourself while I do so."

I wait for Karissa to nod before I grab Adelaide roughly, flipping her over. I wrap her legs around my face. I feel Karissa's irritation at my choice but she is going to learn that despite their patrons, both she *and* Adelaide are mine to do with and what I pleased first. Then, they are eachother's.

❖

ADELAIDE

My hips buck as Josslyn tastes me ever so gently, her lips and tongue barely grazing my clit. She runs her hands up my calves to my thighs before using her fingers to spread my plump lips, exposing my pussy to her eyes completely.

"Mmm, this pussy is so pretty and it's all mine. Do you understand, Adelaide?" Her breath whispers across my clit and I bite my lip. *All hers. Karissa's too,* I add mentally.

Suddenly she is above me, her hand wrapped around my neck, squeezing.

"I expect an answer, Adelaide." She squeezes harder. My pulse thrums throughout my body as she uses her other hand to slap my breasts. Unable to moan, or speak, my eyes roll back until she loosens her hand enough for me to take a shuddering breath.

"Yes, Josslyn, all yours."

I'm not exactly sure how her claim of ownership will work with my responsibilities with the club, but I'm not one to argue with something I desperately want. Josslyn is a force. She is sexy, strong, confident and fucks me better than I could have ever dream of. She gives me pleasure and allows me to give her the same. She is everything I want.

"Good girl," she whispers in my ear, before placing her lips down my neck to my shoulders, then she takes my nipples into her mouth briefly to bite down. My body trembles as she spreads my pussy lips and sucks my clit into her mouth. I arch my back and she wraps her arms around my waist, keeping me in place as she pleases me over and over again.

I lose track of time as she runs her hands all over my body, wringing orgasm after orgasm from my body. But as she keeps going, my lust rises higher and I can't get enough.

I hear a whimper and my head turns to see Karissa writhing in the chair, her eyes blown out and her pussy dripping. I lick my lips, wanting to taste her again, but Josslyn has other plans.

Lifting her head from my pussy, her face dripping in my cum, she beckons Karissa closer.

Grabbing Karissa's face, she kisses her deeply before

rubbing her face over hers. "Mmm, I want you smelling like Adelaide's cum, my sweet girl. I want you to sit on Adelaide's face, facing her feet, my sweet."

As Karissa sits on my face, desperate for release, I grip her tightly and moan in delight while I give her what she most desperately needs… my tongue in her drenched pussy.

❖

KARISSA

I am desperate. Josslyn teased me for over an hour as she fucked Adelaide's pussy with her tongue. So when she calls me, I must stop myself from running over. The taste of Adelaide on Josslyn's tongue is the sweetest candy and I moan into her mouth.

"…sit on Adelaide's face, facing her feet, my sweet girl."

I jump to obey, needing Adelaide's tongue almost more than Josslyn's.

As I sit on her face, I sigh with pleasure, my hips moving seemly on their own as I chase my orgasm.

Josslyn reaches over from behind me and grabs my hair tightly in her grasp. "Right now, both of you are mine to play with. You won't get to play Dom today. I want you to bend and take Adelaide into your mouth, Karissa. While you do, I'm going to fuck that sweet pussy just the way you like and you're going to come for us."

I'm not sure when Josslyn had a chance to put on the strap-on that Jaime had discarded on the bed, now white with Adelaide's dried cum. But as she shoves my face into Adelaide's pussy and Addy sucks my chit into her mouth sharply, she wastes no time in shoving herself inside of my pulsing pussy. I scream in pleasure, the sound muffled as I suck Addy's clit into my mouth.

Daniel was born with a dick and he never knew how to use it like Joss wielded her strap-on. I went through the motions but I never came when he fucked me. I didn't even feel much more than humping. But this? These slow, measured strokes combined with Adelaide's skillful tongue are almost too much pleasure.

Josslyn roughly slaps my ass over and over before grabbing my hips, pushing me back and forth on Adelaide's face while she fucks me. I bite back a scream as the flesh-like dildo slides over my G-spot. I wrap my arms around Adelaide's waist and trail my tongue from her soaked pussy back to her clit, alternating between open-mouth soft kisses and flicking my tongue the way she is doing to me. She moans into my pussy in response and I bite back a scream as she picks up her tempo in response.

Matching her lick for lick and suck for suck, soon we are writhing with our impending orgasms.

"I like that my two favorite girls have been getting along so well. From now on, every night, even if I am not with you, you will fuck each other for me," Josslyn says, grinding herself into me, moaning as the special strap-on stimulates her as well.

"Come for me, girls," she says breathlessly and fucks me harder.

Unable to hold back at her command, Adelaide and I wrap our lips around each other's clits and suck and flick our tongues, wringing out the strongest orgasm of the evening. *Holy fuck.*

KARISSA

I WAKE UP THE NEXT MORNING TO A KNOCK ON MY DOOR.

Groaning, I turn to stuff my head back into my pillow, ignoring the insistent knocking. There is only one person who would bother coming to knock on my door at all. Josslyn would, more than likely, come bursting in without invitation, and Adelaide, more than likely, wouldn't seek me out so soon. If she is feeling anything like I am, she is probably in her bed completely spent. Last night was an explosion of varying sensations and emotional upheavals and damn if it didn't feel amazing. Part of me is dreading finally working with any client, wanting to spend more time with Josslyn as well as Adelaide, as Josslyn wants. The other part of me is excited to explore these parts of my sexuality that I thought were well and truly dead.

My pulse quickens at the thought of seeing Adelaide after Josslyn's demand for us to fuck each other in her absence. I have been reliving that moment until I passed out last night. Part of me genuinely believes she wants us to become closer so that she can have us both without having to split her time more than she has to with her club responsibilities. Now is that because she is starting to like us both? Does she see us going long-term? Or am I projecting and clinging to the possibility that someone could want someone who is as emotionally stunted as I am? Or am I overthinking it all and my boss just enjoys having her cake and eating it too?

"Come in already, Chloe," I shout at the door as the knocking becomes even more incessant.

She comes bounding in with coffee in her hand. "Well, don't you look completely and thoroughly fucked?"

I sit up, snatching the drink from her hand, and take a sip— a balm to my tired soul right now.

"Well, damn. I can come back later if you need a private moment with that cup." Chloe laughs, her eyes a little wide as I slurp down the hot coffee with a vengeance.

"Shut up. I had a late night," I grumble, throwing the sheets back.

"Hmm, I know. Word travels fast around here that Josslyn has two favorite new girls." She comes to sit on the edge of my bed, a smirk on her face, while I pad over to the bathroom.

I grunt in response, my mouth full of toothpaste while I brush my teeth. Not really having an adequate comeback, I took the reprieve. If word is traveling fast that could either mean people are upset or they just like gossip. Neither really appeals to me. Wagging tongues usually mean inaccurate stories and I had enough of that shit growing up. Although *those* particular stories may have been true, it doesn't mean they had to be spread around.

"Don't you want to know what's being said?" Chloe singsongs and I sigh as I leave the bathroom, placing my hands on my hips.

"Should I?" I ask.

"Oh yeah. They're saying that you girls tamed the beast." She giggles and I roll my eyes.

"The beast? Josslyn is not a beast. I am also not sure I can tame anything, let alone someone people consider a beast. That is more of Belle's thing, not mine," I joke and head over to join Chloe. Looking at the clock on my wall, I still have a few hours until I have to, I guess, hunt down my responsibilities for the evening.

"Girl," Chloe scoffs, "I love my boss but she is protective as hell. I can't remember the last time she gave us permission to leave Femme Fatale for a group lunch. I mean, don't get me wrong, we can leave for errands and emergencies but as a group? For a lunch? I mean, we are going to have security and our own section at a really nice posh place across town but"—

I cut her off, "What are you talking about?"

"Oh! That's what I came to tell you before I was distracted by your thoroughly fucked look." She waves at me with a laugh. I roll my eyes. "I came to tell you to get dressed. Josslyn is taking the girls out for a late lunch before we all start work tonight. It will also allow me to introduce you a bit more formally to everyone! We are like one big happy, sex-loving, family."

I turn my head slightly, my eyebrows coming close. "And you're saying she never does this?" I ask, glazing over the last part.

"Other than super special occasions, like a birthday request." Chloe shrugs. "Not really. I mean, you've seen this place. She usually caters events for us and we all party here. Usually, it's not a huge deal for us. We are a very exclusive, hush-hush type of club. The waitlist is a mile long and let's be honest here, Josslyn has cast Femme Fatale very well. A group of women who radiate sexual confidence, grocery shopping while 'Pornhub Pete' and 'sexually-frustrated Susie' argue about different cuts of meat, would certainly grab the attention of the town."

I consider her words. I figure it also wouldn't be the best to run into one of the girl's patrons outside either. I mean, they were sworn to secrecy but I can't imagine everyone being able to keep a straight face all the time. I admit, I also like that Josslyn is protective and caring enough to make sure all of her girls are safe and taken care of. I mean, how many other bosses outfit their employees with full suites, full access to food and drink whenever they want, and with full wardrobes. Not many I imagine. Considering the nature of our "work," protective is good.

"I guess you're right. Still, a change of scenery must be good for everyone too. Okay, what should I wear? How posh is posh?" I ask, jumping out of my bed for the second time that morning. I take in her outfit for the first time—low-cut deep-pink blouse paired with leather pants and high-heeled boots, paired with artfully styled waves in her short hair. Her outfit screamed sexy yet unattainable.

She smiles mischievously. "Oh, you let me play in your new wardrobe. I'll pick out a smoking-hot outfit for your new *lovers* and we can meet the girls at the front entrance in about half an hour." She looks at her watch, jumps up to shove me toward the bathroom, and slams the door behind me. I hear her clap with glee as she finally opens up my new wardrobe. Josslyn had a few more pieces delivered after we had gone shopping, and it certainly was impressive. I sigh as I get into the shower. *Here's hoping for a fun afternoon with no surprises.*

I really need to stop hoping for shit, because clearly that just isn't in my cards. One pair of high silver booties and a long black dress with long sleeves and a slit up the side, full face of makeup later, the excitement of the girls is palpable as we pull up to a restaurant that screams "our entrées cost more than your weekly rent." Although I suppose, the ridiculously lavish limousine we pull up in screams in the same tone "filthy rich." If any part of me questions just how much money Josslyn has as the club owner of an exclusive female pleasure club, that part is punched thoroughly in the face and silenced. A lot is the answer. Obscene is the second answer.

On the way over here, Adelaide sat at my side and I discretely rubbed the small of her back. The girls were laughing and sharing stories good-naturedly while sipping mimosas. After Chloe introduced everyone, it was hard not to join in with their joy and genuine comradery. I did wonder, briefly how the dynamics would be between everyone but it turns out, being thoroughly pleasured and giving pleasure every day really mellowed a woman out. There was not one hint of catty behavior and I was relieved.

In total, including myself, there are eight of us. Caterina, a beautiful Asian woman, with a seemingly permanent salacious smirk on her face. Trisha is her opposite as she is curvier with Native American features and has a Sunday schoolteacher air about her. Then came Lejla, who sends shivers down my spine in spite of myself. Her sharp, ice-blue eyes give no hint of her thoughts, and her distinctive, heavy Slavic accent paired with her husky voice promises pain. If it wasn't for her smile, laugh and sense of humor that seemed to light up everyone around her, I would have considered her a harbinger of death. Part of me is interested to see how she gets on with her patrons, but something tells me that her particular form of pleasure isn't something I could handle. Then there is Rachel, a petite Latina with a light Spanish accent much like Jaime's, who is Adelaide's best friend. Except where Jaime is tall, with long curly hair, tattoos from the neck down with a beautiful caramel complexion, Rachel is short, with shapely thighs and virgin skin that is pale ivory. Jaime also has a distinctive dominant air about her and Rachel reminds me a lot of myself, minus the excessive innocence from my upbringing.

We step out onto the curb and Adelaide finds her way back to me with a smile I easily return. The girls' excitement grows as we follow the maître d' up a curved staircase with gleaming, gold banisters. I blow out a breath as my heels sink into the thick carpet as we make our way to the far side of the restaurant that is filled with people. People's curious gazes follow our group as we make our way inside. Considering the price tag this place must have, a large group would certainly raise a few eyebrows.

"When Jaime said we were going out to a late lunch, I have to admit, I wasn't expecting this," Adelaide's husky voice whispers in my ear.

I bite back a shiver as lust shoots down my spine and I clear my throat. "Chloe said it was a posh place but I have definitely changed my interpretation of the word," I whisper back.

"Ms. Adelaide and Ms. Karissa," the maître d calls out softly, getting our attention. "Ms. Josslyn has requested for both of you to sit here." He points to two chairs on either side of the head of the table. The girls giggle as Adelaide and I make our way and sit at the assigned chairs.

"Girl... I'm not sure what magic you two have wielded but keep it up. I can get used to this." A girl who introduced herself earlier as Caterina smiles at us. She points toward the window view of the marina in front of us and sighs dramatically.

"You act as if your ass isn't drinking champagne worth thousands every night." Chloe shoves Caterina's shoulder with a laugh.

"Okay, okay. But the view?" Caterina rolls her eyes.

"Definitely, but I will tell you... I do *not* envy you two at all," a petite girl named Rachel adds and there are murmurs of agreement.

I frown and look at Adelaide who shrugs her shoulders, confused as well.

"What is that supposed to mean?" I ask, trying to keep the ire from my tone. It's only a few days but I already feel slightly protective of Josslyn.

Rachel laughs. "Oh, nothing bad. Down girl! We all interviewed with Josslyn and had some training. But as amazing as she is, in and out of bed," she adds with a smirk, fanning her face. The girls laugh with a nod. "She is *intense*. I can't imagine catching her attention for too long. I can speak for all of us, I think, except maybe you and Adelaide, that we would probably die from the type of pleasure that woman causes. Nope. I am happy with my patrons."

I laugh and share a smile with Adelaide as everyone nods emphatically. "Josslyn is intense. In the best of ways, though. I can't say I'm sorry you're all happy not having her attention. Adelaide and I will take it," I say with a confidence that surprises me. But I can't say that the words aren't true. I am happy that they don't think of Josslyn as more than a really great boss. I don't want to share her form of pleasure with anyone other than Adelaide. Our chemistry is downright explosive and after months of a hidden sex life followed by a shitty excuse for a relationship, I want to revel in it and in her.

A hush falls in the room and the hairs on my arm suddenly stand at attention. My body feels electrified. I turn my head to watch as Josslyn walks into the restaurant, dressed to the nines in a form-fitting suit and high heels. The looks of lust from both the men and women in the room are downright comical, but Josslyn ignores the looks and the whispers, striding confidently to our table.

"Oh yeah, Adelaide and Karissa have got it bad," Caterina whispers loudly and the girls at the table laugh. I tear my eyes from Josslyn to look at Adelaide with a smile, a look of longing on her face that I'm sure mirrors my own. Fuck it. If I am going to hell, I will do it while I rode Josslyn's face the entire way there, my tongue deep in Adelaide's pussy.

Chapter Fifteen

JOSSLYN

"I SHOULD HOPE SO. IT WOULDN'T BEHOOVE ME TO BE THE owner of a pleasure club if I couldn't grasp the attention of two such gorgeous creatures," I say with a laugh, coming into the tail-end of their conversation. I lean forward to place a kiss on Karissa's lips before moving to do the same to Adelaide.

"Oooooooo," the girls' chorus, and I laugh, signaling the server for another round of drinks and the menus.

I smile as Karissa and Adelaide share a look, their cheeks slightly pink with the desire I just shot through them with a kiss. I'm not one to take adventures outside of the club with the women but I was hit with the urge to show off both Adelaide and Karissa. While I don't have to bring all the other women to do so, the urge was so uncharacteristic, that I invited everyone else as well. If only to attempt, and fail, to convince myself that my obsession with these two girls is anything other than a passing fancy. I am several hundred years old and while I have had several fly-by-night romances, as is in my nature, I never have had the urge to make anyone wholly mine. Well, in this case, as mine as they could be while still working in the club. Admittedly, I wouldn't stop them from pursuing the full power of their sexuality and the self-confidence that comes from that. Women are meant to encourage one another, never to hold each other back. It is counter-productive to evolution.

"Ladies, a toast to our new cast members. May our family continue to thrive," I hold up a glass and a chorus of "here, here" follows.

"I've heard you all use 'cast' quite a bit. Is there a particular reason?" Karissa asks.

"Originally, we had more of a burlesque type of feel. When you walked into the club, I'm sure you noticed the stage and some of the dancers' cages. Eventually, we started to branch out a bit more to become what you see today. While a lot of our girls don't necessarily put on a show, since I make sure that our ladies are doing what they are comfortable with before I give assignments, our patrons like to believe they are. Whether it appeases their conscience when they go home to their loveless marriages or when they justify the expenses to their bosses, I do not know. Nor do I care, as long as in the long run my girls are happy at Fatale and the patrons keep coming back because they are happy too," I explain.

"Yeah, you may notice that some of the clubgoers that aren't part of the patron list will ask for a certain one of us and they will say 'Cast Member Karissa,' for example," Trisha chimes in.

Karissa nods. "Okay, so everyone at this table has patrons."

"Yes, everyone at this table does. However, as you know, there are girls who work for Fatale who simply dance, private or otherwise. Those girls don't work with anyone in particular. That is reserved for the more... proficient of our girls."

"If you don't mind me asking, Joss. Why not hire in-house?" Adelaide asks, leaning forward, her eyes wide. Her vulnerability is like a punch in the gut and it makes me want to grab her and take her to a room where I can replace the look with one of lust.

"The girls that join in a dancer capacity make it clear that it is their limit. Enticing through dance and providing that kind of escape is its own talent. I cannot fault anyone for being attached to their art form. Our art form is a bit more physical in nature, but it is still an art, nonetheless. It takes a special type of paintbrush to bring pleasure to our patrons and we wield it, oh so well." I smile and the ladies let off a soft, quiet cheer. Even so, the other customers of the restaurant turn to stare blatantly. But we tend to have that effect when we go out of the club setting.

I usually avoid it for multiple reasons but the most important reason is that these women all live under the influence of a succubus twenty-four-seven. Although they may not have my powers of lust and enticement, they benefit from it in that they become a lot more alluring than the average human. All these women are already beautiful in their own right, but after prolonged exposure, they have a certain electric radiance that captivates the senses and penetrates every defense. In short, they are downright irresistible. This is why, although they may not realize it, I have various security measures in place, me being here with them, their first layer of defense. Alone, my strength and speed are enough to take out a small army.

The food arrives and everyone starts to tuck into their plates. I give them all a few minutes before I turn to Adelaide and Karissa as they finish. "Ladies, you'll find that when we go back to the club, I took the liberty of having your rooms changed. Your suites are now located in a set of apartments next to mine. You'll still have your own rooms and bath, but you'll have a shared living space as well. On your beds, I have laid out your assignments that start tonight," I say softly.

"Why the room change?" Adelaide asks and I frown at her. She quickly looks away.

"There is a difference between curiosity-based questions about the club and those based on questioning my decisions. I do not need a reason to move your room. I want you closer to me to do with as I wish, when I wish. I want to be able to hear you scream in pleasure when you are both together," I say, my tone low and laced with a pulse of my power. I see their eyes dilate and their delicate tongues wet their lips.

"Now, my sweet Addy, I have better ways for you to use that sweet mouth. Since it is time for dessert, why don't you go under the table and give Karissa a sweet preview of what it will be like when it's just you two together?"

Adelaide's breathing turns shallow at the request, her desire to please weaving with her lust. It is intoxicating. Karissa swallows thickly and moves her chair further into the table where her entire lower half is covered by the long tablecloth. Karissa's eyes shift around the table as Adelaide moves into position between her legs, but I could have told her they would pay us no mind. We were a pleasure club after all.

❖

ADELAIDE

I lick my lips in anticipation as I run my hands up Karissa's dress, hiking it up around her waist. Pulling her hips closer, I leave her thin panties on for now and kiss her throbbing pussy over and over. She squirms a bit and I respond by pulling her panties up, enough to apply pressure to her clit while I run my mouth and tongue up and down her soaking slit and swollen lips. So sweet. I don't know why I questioned Josslyn but part of me knew she would issue the best type of punishment. Honestly, being slightly cheeky for the chance to taste the sweetest of pussies is worth it. Sure, I could technically do this with Karissa whenever I want, but I prefer being told what to do and when to do it. It heightens the pleasure for me. I appreciate that Josslyn recognizes that in me, and doesn't make me feel tawdry for it.

I quickly pull Karissa's panties off, taking advantage of her squirming hips. Bringing my face closer, I close my eyes as I suck her swollen clit into my mouth gently, applying just the barest of pressure with my tongue while I suck. I hear her hiss in pleasure and Josslyn's muffled laugh. Suddenly Karissa sits up straighter and I hear a muffled conversation. With my head between her thighs, the conversation is muffled but sensing her distress, I tug her hips back gently and increase the speed of my tongue ever so slightly, alternating moving my lips back and forth against her soaking pussy. One hand finds its way under the table and she wraps my hair in her grasp gently. I smile against her and I increase my tempo and suck her clit into my mouth, in response. No longer teasing her, I push two fingers inside her and curl them slightly, working her G-spot as I suck and lick her. Her hips move ever so slightly, desperate for release as I keep her on the edge and whatever conversation is being held above me continues. Her movements become more frantic and her other hand joins the first as she pulls me closer to her core. I was sure at this point whoever is nearby and cares to look would be able to tell that Karissa is being pleasured thoroughly under the table. So I bite down gently on her clitoris, fuck her harder with my hand and increase the speed of my tongue and lips. Her pussy clamps down and despite the lack of clear sound, I make out a gasp and gentle moan as a rush of her sweetness coats my tongue. I withdraw my hand but take my time lapping up her juices, savoring her smooth pussy, knowing that it will be hours until I'm back between her thighs again.

I slip out from underneath the table and come face-to-face with two furious, yet lust-filled faces. Before I can think, Josslyn grabs my hand, still sticky with Karissa's juices, and sucks my fingers clean.

"Nice of you to rejoin us, my sweet girl. My, my, but Karissa tastes so much sweeter on your fingers," Josslyn says with a moan before flicking an icy gaze to the two people who are watching the scene unfold. "I believe you two were leaving now. Karissa said what she had to say. You're not welcome nor needed in her life anymore. It will be in your best interest to walk away while you still have legs to help you do that." she looks toward the corner and security seemingly steps out of the shadows.

With a huff, the lady turns on her heel and the guy follows with a sneer, though the look of lust as they walk away is unmistakable.

"What did I miss?" I ask softly and Josslyn laughs. Karissa gives me a look and I'm sure she would let me in on everything later.

Chapter Sixteen

KARISSA

I SWALLOW THICKLY, TRYING TO CONTROL MY BREATHING AS Adelaide settles herself between my thighs, hiking up my dress from underneath the table. My eyes flick around, just to see if anyone else saw Adelaide disappear under the table.

Josslyn chuckles. "Relax, Karissa. Even if anyone saw our sweet Addy go under the table, with this crowd…" she looks around the room and I follow her gaze, squirming in my seat while Addy kisses me through my panties, taking in the expensive outfits and haughty faces that scream, "rich and pretentious."

"With this crowd, anyone who saw would burn with jealousy, counting down the minutes until they can make up an excuse to fuck their mistresses, chasing only a tenth of the pleasure that you're about to feel from our girl's sweet mouth," her voice purrs. She watches me with an intensity that is almost corporal as it caresses me. She smirks before taking a sip of her wine and I hiss in pleasure as Adelaide gets my panties off and sucks my clit between her lips.

Josslyn lets out a low chuckle.

"Karissa? It is you!" I feel my back straighten as a familiar voice comes from behind me. *God, no.*

I turn my head as Lacey appears next to me, smiling brightly. Josslyn raises an eyebrow, her gaze curious.

"Lacey?"

"Oh, shit," Annie breathes from her spot at the table and I feel the girls focus on us.

From her side, Leija picks up a steak knife, caressing it almost gently. "Should we…" her husky voice trails off, the coldness leaving a trail of malice that leaves no question about what she meant. My heart warms at how quickly she came to my defense… even if it was in a violent way.

Josslyn looks at her sharply. "Leija." One word and Leija nods in answer and smiles. At Josslyn's nod, the girls turn back to their conversations, although I know they have one ear to our side of the table.

"Lacey… is an old friend," I answer Josslyn's curious stare, trying to keep my face blank as Adelaide continues to work me over with her ridiculously talented mouth.

"Hmm, I see." Josslyn chuckles lightly.

"I think we are more than old friends, Karissa," Lacey responds, a slight frown on her face.

I look at her up and down. She's wearing a short, tight gold dress, Louboutins on her feet, her hair styled perfectly and diamonds rounding off her look. I bite back a scoff until I hear a throat clear and my eyes fall on, none other than Daniel standing next to her.

"We were," I shrug. "Until you left me to fend for myself,

choosing to go to church camp to absolve you of your sins while I had to leave home."

"I had to go. My parents were going to disown me. I tried to get better but I couldn't stop thinking about you. When I went back, you were gone. I focused on being healthy instead." Her face flushes red as she talks, her eyes flicking toward Daniel.

Josslyn laughs. "Daniel, so nice to see you again. Tell us, did your girlfriend from the mall decide, just like my sweet Karissa, that she preferred women instead of... you?"

I feel my mind unraveling as I reach one hand under the table discreetly, wrapping my hand in Adelaide's hair to bring her closer.

"*Your* sweet..." Lacey starts, her face taking on a look I don't think I've ever seen on her. But it's gone so quickly I can almost believe I imagined it if it didn't fill me with unease.

Daniel's face goes red with anger and he ignores Josslyn and looks at Lacey. "What is she talking about, Lacey?"

Oh my God, Adelaide. I reach my other hand under the table, wrapping it in her hair to join the first, not really caring about whatever the fuck is going on around me as my hips move imperceptibly, chasing everything Adelaide is giving me. Although I admit, the distraction is allowing me to drag this out as much as possible.

Lacey looks at Daniel. "Just because I'm being forced to marry you, doesn't mean you can question me or judge me." She looks back at me. "You were always meant to be mine. Are you okay?"

Josslyn's eyes sparkle. "Oh, Karissa is more than okay. I would say she is almost *orgasmically* happy."

"Jesus, fuck," Daniel mumbles, shifting to hide his growing hard-on as he looks toward the bottom of the table as if he could see through it.

"Karissa..." Lacey begins, her eyes flicking between Josslyn, my expression, and the table.

"Let me make this perfectly clear." I gasp lightly and my eyes grow heavy. Trying to focus, I clear my throat. "Lacey, I don't care about whatever trip you want to take down memory lane. I stopped thinking about you the moment I left that shitty town. I have everything and one…" I look at Joss quickly, "that I want. It's not you."

Lacey's face turns red, but I continue, needing to get this out before I lose my mind with pleasure and my ability to speak. I look at Daniel. "Daniel, I hope you know your fiancée was eating my pussy every chance she got. So that makes what? Three women in just under seventy-two hours who prefer actual skill over none? How does it feel to know that when you go to bed with your fiancée, it will be my pussy she remembers while you grunt over her bored body? You both disgust me, so you both deserve each other. You can go now. I'm in the middle of face fucking one of my girlfriends and her mouth is… So. Fucking. Talented." I moan out the last and the girls' snigger and Josslyn smirks.

Adelaide bites my clit and curls her fingers just right and I gasp as I toss my head back with a moan as I come all over her lips. She gently laps up all my cream. Moments later, Adelaide comes out from the other side of the table, looking put together, her lips slightly swollen, glistening with my cream. I look at her with pure lust, ignoring the two assholes behind me. Fuck them. I know what I want, and it isn't a history lesson. It's Josslyn, Adelaide, and my new family at Femme Fatale.

KARISSA

I FELT LIKE WAS FLOATING THE ENTIRE WAY BACK TO THE CLUB, AT peace even as the girls recounted the story to Adelaide. I felt like I closed the door on two chapters of my life and embraced something that finally felt… right.

Adelaide and I make our way over to our new suite, right next to Josslyn's. Remembering the way here, I don't need to ask for directions and I am grateful for it. I feel like I am home.

Grabbing Adelaide's hand, we unlock the door with the key Josslyn pressed into each of our hands before going to her office. We push the doors open and pause at the pure opulence of the room.

"Wow," she breathes. I nod, my jaw slightly unhinged as we step in, the door falling closed behind us with an audible click as it self-locks.

The living room area is a miniature version of the club lounge, with deep purple oversized couches paired with a thick plush black carpet. The room is furnished with gold-and-white accent pieces. To the right is a fully equipped open floor plan kitchen with gold appliances.

"This is insane," I mutter in awe.

"Wait until you see the rooms." Adelaide's voice comes from the other side of the suite where there are two doors that presumably lead into the bedrooms. Following her voice, I peer into the rooms that are almost identical to our old rooms, except they are double the size and had a walk-in wardrobe as well as an en suite. The rooms have a connecting door leading to the other and I smile. This is perfect.

Adelaide goes to sit on the edge of the bed, picking up a heavy, embroidered envelope with her name written in script. Her assignments. She looks up at me with a small smile. "Want to open ours together?"

"Let me go grab it." I grin and run through the connecting doors to grab my envelope off my bed before returning to Adelaide.

Sitting on the edge of the bed, we open the envelopes and bring the first of three notes together. I breathe a sigh of relief when I see they are identical.

On heavy stationary paper, inscribed are two names with the room number we would be in as well as the days and times notated next to those names; *Myia Day (Monday and Thursday, 3-7) Patron Room 3, and Mrs. Alicia Janet (Tuesday and Fridays, 5-9Monday and Thursday, 3-7) Patron Room 6.* I look at the time, noting that we have about an hour before we need to make our way to where we have to go.

Placing that first paper down we look at the next, which is also identical.

MYIA DAY (26 YEARS OF AGE)

Fatales
Adelaide, Jaime, Karissa

Sexual Preferences and Directives
This patron likes variety in her sexual preferences.
Communication is key to determining her current sexual mood and needs.
If the patron chooses to be dominant, Adelaide and Karissa can take point.
If the patron chooses to be submissive, Jaime will take control with Karissa to assist.
If the patron chooses to explore both sides, all Fatales will participate.

Preferred Outfits of her Fatales
Patron prefers Fatales to be fully clothed upon arrival, hair styled down.
During the session, Patron would prefer full nudity.
Patron has requested to dress and leave the room before Fatales.

Hard Stops
The patron will absolutely not engage in any anal play nor see it performed.
Patron has requested absolutely no wielded sexual tools that can cause any pain or imprisonment including but not limited to; clamps, whips, chains, handcuffs, collars, and similar items.

In the case that the patron shows interest, she must fully verbalize her request by approaching the security camera located inside the room. (Patrons have agreed to security cameras onsite, for safety. All footage is deleted after twenty-four hours for privacy and can only be accessed by club owner, Josslyn.

ALICIA JANET

Fatales
Adelaide, Karissa

Sexual Preferences and Directives
This Patron is Dominant
Silence is requested unless spoken to

Preferred Outfits of her Fatales
No clothes are preferred at all times.

Hard Stops
The patron will never be submissive.
No tools, or toys

Patron has been informed of all contractual obligations as well as the sexual preferences of her Fatales. No intentional cruelty or physical abuse will be tolerated against Fatales. As set by the contracts, Patrons are also protected from unwanted abuse or physical contact. In the case of abuse, there will be immediate intervention as well as swift punishment onsite.

We blow out a breath after reading through the second note.

"What do you think?" Adelaide asks.

I pause for a moment and consider my response. On one hand, if Adelaide is with me, I feel that we could get through it. On the other hand, I'm not looking forward to being submissive to anyone other than Josslyn. I spent my entire life submissive to everyone else's whims. With Josslyn, I crave her. Something about her just puts me on edge while still giving me a sense of comfort. That combination is intense. With Adelaide, I want to taste her vulnerability on my tongue. I feel comfortable being more in control. Having her give me that level of trust is humbling. Myia, by the looks of her card, is going to be a walk in the park but Mrs. Janet? I'm not too sure about it.

"Myia will probably be a good fit for our dynamics. But Mrs. Janet? I'm not sure yet how I will be able to…" I trail off.

"Hmm, I know what you mean." She lies down on the bed and I turn my body to lie down, propping my head on my hand, and looking down at her gorgeous face.

"You do?" I question, my eyebrow slightly raised.

"Yes. While I am naturally submissive it still makes me nervous when I have new sexual partners. Not everyone knows how to… treat a submissive well. Just because we enjoy pleasing our partners doesn't mean that they can push us past our comfort zones. But some Doms break you down emotionally until you are going way past that point of comfort just because you're aching to please them in anyway. Maybe one more orgasm, maybe a few more hits of the paddle. Then, you can give it your all and they still don't praise you and you feel less than worthless. Because now, you're worthless and broken and you hurt so badly that you just want to escape but you stay and hope that you can just be better next time." Adelaide's eyes take on a faraway look as a tear leaks out the corner of her eye.

My heart breaks at her words and I reach up to wipe the tear from her face. "You are safe now. I will never abuse your trust. Josslyn won't either. If we hate Janet, Josslyn will make sure she's a memory. C'mon, let's shower and get ready for Myia."

She smiles warmly, reaching to grab my hand, giving it a small squeeze. As we move, the third letter falls.

"Oh, it's from Josslyn," I mutter and I read it aloud.

My sweet girls, my good girls,
as you can already tell you will only be assigned

two patrons and you will be staying together.
Although this is business, take your pleasure but never
give more of yourself than you are willing and able to.
*   Watch over one another but know I am always*
watching and you two are always safe.

Josslyn

oth of the letters are identical and we both smile.

"Well, there you see it. Looks like our... Josslyn... has it all covered." I grin as we make our way to our respective bathrooms. I can't help but think, what *is* Josslyn to us? How do we put a label on it and do we even need one?

KARISSA

To say that I am nervous about tonight is a complete understatement. While I am happy that I would be with Adelaide, there is something in the pit of my stomach that is screaming, "run." First-time jitters maybe, but I can't be sure. Regardless, holding Adelaide's hand and giving it a squeeze, I take a deep breath as we stood outside Patron Room 6.

Walking into the room, Mrs. Janet is sitting on a large circular bed outfitted with black sheets, already fully naked, legs crossed, as she holds a glass full of amber, colored liquor. On the wall are a variety of handcuffs, strap-ons, and various-sized dildo attachments to match. Closing the door behind us, she smiles, her eyes glinting with desire. It sets me on edge.

"Ladies, let's not waste time here. I want to take advantage of these four hours. Adelaide, I believe we have met before.

Well," she laughs lightly, "you've met my cunt before, in the boardroom."

Adelaide nods hesitantly.

"Ah, good. You know my wishes then. Silence unless requested. That goes for moaning as well. Adelaide, I want your mouth on my pussy. Karissa, you must kneel at my head, hands crossed until I ask you to move. Nod if you understand, then begin."

We do.

Adelaide settles herself between Janet's now open legs while I kneel at her head.

She ignores me and pours some of the alcohol on her pussy. "Lap that up, whore," she commands and Adelaide bends to lick her from ass to clit while Janet tosses her head back in pleasure.

❖

JANET

As Adelaide settles herself between my legs, I admire her curves. She is every bit as beautiful as she was in the exhibition room. My heart races as I think of everything I am going to make her do. She is going to be my little toy. I ignore Karissa. She isn't what I want. She lacks the vulnerability of Adelaide and I feel a stab of rage flow through me at the thought... I will enjoy making Karissa submit to me, eventually.

But first, I take the whiskey and pour some on my throbbing pussy. "Adelaide, lap that up, whore. Get every drop and eat me until I ask you to stop."

I hiss as she quickly dips her head, licking me ass to clit before sucking my clit into her luscious mouth. *Fuck.* Just as good as I remember. I grab her head roughly with one hand, groaning as I push her face closer as she uses her pouty lips, flicking gently with the tip of her tongue.

"Yes, your mouth is fucking talented. You little slut. Mmm, taste me." I thrust my hips, closing my legs around her face to keep in her place. She is going nowhere until she makes me cum several times over. To make up for each time my ridiculous husband tried and failed to fuck me well. It is pitiful really. But here? I am the boss. These two will fuck me and suck me and be fucked by me until I grow tired of them.

I moan as my first orgasm rolls through my body.

"Fuck, yes. You little slut. You better eat this pussy like it was fucking made for you to eat. Lie the fuck down. I'm going to ride your fucking face." Pulling her away, she lies on her back, looking breathless and I smirk. All mine.

I settle myself on her face. "Begin. Karissa, kneel, legs open at Adelaide's head. You're going to lick this whiskey off my tits." I pour the rest of the liquid down my chest slowly, watching it dribble down my belly to my pussy as Adelaide laps it up.

I smile as Karissa leans over and licks her way up my breasts, sucking my nipples. "That's right, Karissa. You do what I ask. Suck harder, you little bitch," I say softly and she does what I ask. I'll start slow with Karissa until she can't sleep from the pain of me spanking her smooth, creamy ass.

I feel a rush of power as they follow my directives. This goes beyond the office. There, everyone jumps because I run the company, but right now? They jump because I tell them to please me, to make me come because my husband can't. I love it and I want to see how far I can take it.

Grabbing Adelaide's head, I grin as I ride her tongue, feeling an orgasm building. "Yes, fuck my clit, you little slut. I'm going to fucking drown you with my cum. Lap it up. Yes. Fuck, yes!" I scream as an orgasm tingles from my toes to my head and back. A rush of liquid pours from my pussy as I bounce on

Adelaide's face, Karissa sucking my nipples into her mouth, rolling them with her tongue. I climb off and slump over slightly as I recover. I have never come so damn hard and I certainly have never squirted.

I look on almost ferally as Adelaide lies on the bed, coated in my juices. I like her like that, ready for me to continue to use.

"Get on all fours, Adelaide. Karissa, you are to kneel and watch."

Karissa nods as she settles herself in front of Adelaide. I get up and walk over to the wall of specialized strap-ons and insert it inside of me before I adjust the straps. I pick a large, thick dildo, wanting to see Adelaide's perfect pink-and-chocolate pussy stretch for me while I fuck her senseless. If I can make her scream and disobey my request for silence, I can punish her and fuck her in her tight little rim.

I walk back and pause as I take in the scene. Her sweet plump ass in the air matches her plump chocolate pussy lips, her pink core on display for me. As beautiful as Karissa is, with her perfect breasts and striking green eyes, something about Adelaide is driving me into a frenzy. I want her at my mercy more than I think I have ever wanted anything before.

❖

KARISSA

Janet's voice is pitched higher, her breath quickening as her eyes take on an almost fanatic shine. My heart twinges and I feel unsettled in more ways than one. This is beyond the burn of jealousy. In truth, being slightly jealous is something I expected and I braced myself for it. Part of the appeal of working at the club was exploration and I appreciated it, however, I also wasn't expecting to have this connection with one of my coworkers let alone our boss.

Taking solace that Josslyn is watching in some capacity, I kneel and wait as requested, even if the command makes me chafe. As Janet grabs a larger-than-average dildo, my body goes rigid. When her stare becomes more intense and her chest heaves that unease doubles. My eyes flick toward the blinking camera and I have to wonder if Josslyn feels the increase in Janet's frenzied emotions. She is almost becoming unhinged and I'm not sure if it is part of her sexual and emotional needs or if she truly is unraveling.

She starts to pace, holding the large dildo in place as the weight of it makes it flop. "You know, for years I have been at the beck and call of my husband when we are in the bedroom. I dealt with it. After all, growing up, my mom would drill into my head that I had a duty—remain chaste, marry for the connections it would bring, and strengthen our investments. I was never allowed even a boyfriend, and no one would come near me with a ten-foot pole, too afraid that my family would bankrupt theirs." She scoffs.

"My husband, Archibald, is twenty years my senior. I knew him while I grew up. What kind of a name is Archibald? Fucking stupid, that's what kind of name." She mutters the last. "He would give me lavish gifts for my birthday, the holidays, and the like. When I started high school, he started showing up with flowers after school. My friends were so jealous. I had a handsome older man while they were dealing with arrogant, trust-fund toting, high school boys. They had no idea that as I got older, the preverbal noose around my neck would tighten. Sure he was handsome, but I wanted to be normal, date and go to parties, not be taken to lavish dinners. I guess I was fortunate enough to be a late bloomer as eventually, his stares went from sweet to... lascivious. His comments and questions went from innocent ones to asking if I played with my pussy at night. Telling me to dream of him and his dick stretching 'my tight little pussy.'" Her posture is stiff. She tries and fails to wrap her hand around the dildo, her hand barely covering half.

She walks toward Adelaide and strokes her ass, almost lovingly. "It was disgusting. But despite my pleas to my father, at eighteen I was making my way down the aisle. Imagine that, eighteen years old married to a thirty-eight-year-old man who leaped at the chance to fuck a tight, young, virgin pussy, pawing at my body like a savage. The dinners eventually stopped. If he wasn't working, he would come home to use my body as he saw fit. Sometimes even in front of the servants. They would even serve our food, while he groaned and swore loudly as he shoved his dick down my throat from under the table. My food would get cold, while his cum would fill my throat. Eventually, he started having the female servants join us. They loved it too. See, to them, a hot aristocrat was pounding away at their pussies while his wife watched. They got a kick out of it when he would make me eat their pussy while he fucked me from behind. Jokes on him though, I had a sweet little servant eating my pussy when he wasn't home and making me come when he couldn't." She smacks Adelaide's pussy and she sighs in pleasure.

"So obedient. Just like my servants. I loved that, you know. The rush from making them do what I wanted, in order for them to keep their jobs. I would even record it. Insurance." She shrugs as if her preying on her servants was normal. Yes, this bitch is absolutely fucking crazy.

She sighs loudly, running her hands over Adelaide's waist and tummy and then squeezing her breasts roughly. "Mmm, fucking perfect. He monitored my diet too, made sure I kept going to the gym. As my body matured and my curves were more pronounced, he became even more... invested in keeping my body perfect."

Her voice becomes more breathless as she speaks, her hands

caressing before she goes to stand behind Adelaide, dipping two fingers inside her, drawing up her plump lips before pinching her clitoris.

Licking her fingers clean with a moan, her eyes flutter closed. "So damn sweet. I wonder what your diet is like. You'll have to keep it up. I'm a bit bitter and I hate tasting myself from my husband's dick when he shoves it back in my mouth to clean it off after sex. I hate him."

Janet's body almost vibrates with tension as she walks over to the small table that holds a decanter. She fills up a new glass with the amber liquid, her previous cup discarded on the bed. Adelaide remains on all fours as directed and our gazes meet, apprehension flashing in her eyes as Janet chugs her drink and pours another, bringing it to her lips. Her tangent takes on a fever pitch, her hands moving frantically, making her drink splash over and drip to the floor.

"When I took over my father's company a few years later, it was nice, you know? Running things, making sure the business grew. It was the only time I had true control other than the whore servants. My father, despite his archaic ideas about marriage arrangements, ensured that it was one hundred percent mine. No shareholders, no one to answer to. My husband couldn't even have a say and he still doesn't. Oh, he tries, but he has his own company to run, one that my father's company has shares of. He knows my father would freeze him out if he tried to intervene."

Swaying slightly, cheeks bright red, she finishes her drink and tosses the glass across the room. I jump slightly as it shatters against the wall.

Her words slur almost a whisper as she continues, "You know... no you wouldn't." She giggles. "Just yesterday, he had me come into his office for lunch. After, he had me bent over his desk, groaning loudly as he fucked me. His assistant came in, announcing a meeting before she froze. She apologized but he waved her off, telling her to send them in. 'Get under my desk and suck me off like a good little wife,' he said. He isn't a quiet lover. He gets off by being loud and saying disgusting things to me. His business associates laughed as the conversation bounced back and forth between, 'that's right, slurp all over my dick, whore,' to 'the merger will be a good idea.' After he came he had me get up and I had to walk out of his office with his associates still there. It was degrading."

Janet drags the dildo up and down Adelaide's slit. "I can see the appeal now, sweet Addy. You're *my* little whore to use as I want and Karissa here is going to watch just like his business associates did as Archibald fucked me on his desk yesterday. So stay just like that, Adelaide. I am going to make that pretty, tight-looking pussy, mine," Janet says, her voice pitched dangerously low, letting out a moan of pleasure as the strap-on switches on.

"I even chose a nice big one. You'll scream for me and then I'll have to punish you. I'll fuck your tight little asshole then." She shudders.

My eyes widen at her words, my breath shaky. *This woman is certifiable.* Fuck that, this isn't happening. Janet has no concept of how to be a true dominant. She is a sadist. Her history of negative sexual experiences may have twisted her into the person she is right now but it is absolutely no excuse for abuse.

Quickly, I get off the bed and shove her away from Adelaide. "Get the fuck away from Addy, you crazy bitch," I snarl, getting up close and personal. Adelaide scrambles off the bed to stand behind me.

It takes Janet a few seconds before she grins, strikes my face with the open palm of her hand, and snarls, "I'm going to enjoy breaking you, you little bitch. Now, I'll get the pleasure of punishing your worthless little ass. I paid for this membership. You are mine to use."

She laughs maniacally while my ears ring from her slap.

Almost faster than my eyes can follow, Josslyn is suddenly there, her hands wrapped around Janet's neck. At least I think it's Josslyn. I stare transfixed as Adelaide's hand clutches mine and we edge slightly around the scene, to get a better view or to get out of the range of what is to come, I wasn't sure.

Adelaide and I look at each other briefly before turning back to the scene, speechless as we take in a slightly larger, more muscular version of our Josslyn. But that isn't what has our jaws unhinged. No, it was the shiny obsidian, curled horns, now coming out of Josslyn's head, paired with a long-barbed tail that is swishing back and forth in clear agitation. Rounded off with large, deep purple, leather wings and her eyes glowing purple, with a red ring around the irises, Josslyn is fucking terrifyingly beautiful.

JOSSLYN

I STAND ON THE OTHER SIDE OF THE FALSE WALL ALL OF THE
patron rooms have, watching the security footage and listening
in on Mrs.Janet's crazed diatribe. I watch as her movements
became jerky, her breathing borderline causing her to hyper-
ventilate. I know I am going to have to intervene. Something in
my gut told me I may have to kill. Watching the girls in this
situation sparks a bit of jealousy but nothing I can't control.

However, control goes completely out of the realm of possibility as she threatens *my* Adelaide, even more so when her
filthy human hand strikes *my* Karissa. I feel my body shift into
my true form as I burst into the room and wrap my clawed
hand around Janet's neck. I watch as her face becomes a
mottled red as she tries and fails to scream in fear. I breathe in
her fear. While it doesn't feed me, I revel in it. No one will hurt

any of my Fatales but absolutely no one will cause pain to my girls. She will die tonight, of that I am absolutely sure.

My lips turn into a smirk. "Listening to you verbalize your diary was intriguing enough. Your little soliloquy even tugged at my dark heartstrings… until it didn't."

I toss her to the floor and watch as she crawls back on her hands, the ridiculous dildo flapping between her legs.

"What are you?" she asks, her eyes full of tears as she rubs her neck, sobbing.

"I am the person that is going to rip your fucking head from your neck in a few moments. But allow me my own speech, first." I flex my wings as I stalk her across the room.

"You signed a contract Janet," I tsk. "You knew the rules and yet you came into my club with the intention of hurting my girls, my family. You knew the limitations. There was to be no forced pain. Simply put, you fucked up by not reading the invisible fine print. Your life is forfeit when you abuse your power in this room and hurt *anyone* without their express consent." My voice is low as I hover over her body, tears now streaming down her face.

"They are just paid whores," she grates out.

I see red and I rear back and slap her, my claws raking her face. Her tears now combine with blood as her skin flays open.

Her scream is music to my ears. Just like she wanted to hear my sweet Addy scream, I will enjoy while I return that thought with action.

I breathe deeply, the urge to kill her almost reaching a boiling point. "It's a shame that a woman would devalue another woman for their chosen profession and lifestyle. Here at Femme Fatale, we cater to sexual expression and freedom. Dancers or Fatales, we teach every member of our cast that, as long as everyone is of consenting age, they are not to be ashamed of their sexual preferences. but instead, I teach them how to properly wield those predilections to maximize not only their pleasure and happiness but that of their patrons. We encourage trust between our patron and their chosen Fatales. They cultivate a relationship that is mutually beneficial emotionally and physically. Femme Fatale is *not* a sex club, Femme Fatale is *liberation*."

"You can't kill me. My family will look for me." Her voice takes on the frantic air of someone who knows her time of death is drawing near. It is absolutely delicious.

I lick my lips as I reach to grip her neck, cutting off her air supply briefly. "The benefit of being me are my various connections. They won't miss you because they won't know you're gone. Amiera, can you come in here please?" I ask, keeping my eyes on her face. I am rewarded as her face goes slack and a resigned look takes over her features.

"Yes, boss?" a voice tinged with laughter comes from behind me. I laugh as Karissa and Adelaide take in the newcomer, who is an exact clone of Mrs. Janet. Their heads swivel back and forth.

"As I was saying, the benefit of being a demon older than a millennium, such as myself, are all the other demons I have on my payroll. So, no one will realize you are gone because *you won't be.* Amiera is a very convincing shapeshifter, don't you think? The best part? All that money you've come to own will be under my control now. Thank you for the very generous investment." I laugh as I squeeze her neck harder, until my claws rip straight through, her head now detached from her body.

❖

ADELAIDE

While deep inside I knew there was something different about Josslyn, at no point in time did I think that difference would have meant "demon." But it, *she,* isn't scaring me. I still feel that odd sense of comfort when I am in her presence. Even though she does look like a more voluptuous version of the drawn beast figures shown at Sunday school, I know her character.

Even if the spray of blood on her face and growing dark puddle at her feet is a bit unsettling, she isn't. In fact, this fiercer side is… alluring. One look at Karissa and I know she feels the same.

"I don't know, boss. I think the best part will be liberating her staff and teaching her husband several lessons," the Janet replica, newcomer Amiera, says, her hands clapping gleefully.

Josslyn laughs. "I agree. We will discuss the next steps with her company and staff before you head out. You can change back until it's time to go, Amiera. No need for us to see Janet's face more than we must."

In a flash, a petite slim form with pink horns, a pink tail, and an easy smile stands before us, dressed in a mini skirt and matching black low-cut top. She reaches to shake our hands. "Hello. Sorry to meet this way, but I am Amiera, your average demonic shapeshifter." Her tinkling voice is endearing, and we smile.

Josslyn clears her throat and rolls her eyes. "While introductions are wonderful, why don't we get Adelaide and Karissa at least into a robe, so they aren't standing around naked in a murder scene straight out of one of those shows on TV."

Amiera laughs, making two robes appear from thin air. We gape as we grab them, putting them on. "Like Supernatural! Those guys are so hot. I wish I could shape-shift and fuck myself as Dean," she sighs wistfully.

"Hades, help us," Josslyn mutters before turning to us with a smile, her voice uncharacteristically soft. "My sweet girls, while I am sure you have questions, why don't you head over to the suite and let me tie up a few loose ends here? I'll join you after."

KARISSA

Having showered and thrown on a soft robe, Adelaide and I sit on the couch of the suite as we wait for Josslyn to come over.

"I wonder how long it takes to clean up a murder scene and discuss a company takeover," I ask, my eyes flicking to the clock.

Adelaide laughs and I grin and then join in.

"Not sure but I hope she comes over in her demon form." She giggles.

I find myself nodding in agreement. I should be shocked but there is something about a crazed, horned Josslyn bursting in to save the day and kill for us, that erases all worries of the unknown. Everyone in the club knows that Josslyn is slightly different. How different, I'm sure they weren't aware of, but I don't think it would matter if they did. Josslyn is… Josslyn—intimidating, demanding, and dominant but attentive, caring, and understanding.

Amiera was a mind fuck, though. I have to wonder how many demons are walking around Femme Fatale. Based on Josslyn's speech I am sure the answer is "a fuck-ton."

I look at Adelaide and turn until I'm facing her directly and reach over to caress her face. "I'm so glad you're okay and that Janet showed her character sooner rather than later. She was unbalanced."

Leaning into my hand, she smiles softly. "Thank you for standing up for me. Other than Jaime, no one has ever cared enough to make sure I was safe. You and Josslyn have shown me more consideration than anyone else has, ever."

Her voice hitches and I lean forward to capture her lips with mine, running my tongue along the seam of her lips until she opens them with a sweet sigh.

Pulling away, I brush my lips against hers with a murmur, "I will never let anyone hurt you. You are mine, Adelaide, every part of you. Let me show you just how much." As I talk, I pull her robe open and lean her back on the large couch, settling between her legs.

I kiss her plump lips, letting them cradle my face as I draw my tongue up her slit until I hit her clit. Using two fingers to separate her lips, I press a kiss onto her sweet nub. Her sweet, soft moan is like music to my ears. Not every instance has to be a sub/Dom dynamic. Sometimes providing comfort to one another is just as important to your relationship. I reach one hand to draw up her body until I softly pinch and twist her nipples while I gently swirl my tongue around her sweet spot before biting down gently and sucking her into my mouth.

Her back arches in pleasure. "Yes, please."

I don't stop as Josslyn's voice comes behind me, focusing on drawing the pleasure out of the sweet pussy in front of me.

"Now this, my sweet girls, taking pleasure from each other, is what I like to see," she says softly. Her figure, also robed, comes into my peripherals as I push two fingers into Adelaide, curling them just right as I gently tease her clit, keeping her on edge.

"Please, let me taste you," Adelaide breathes out, her hands pulling her own hair in pleasure.

"Well, when you ask so sweetly how can I say no?" Josslyn drops her robe and settles over Adelaide's face, moaning softly as Adelaide wraps her hands around Josslyn's waist, breathing in deeply and licking her slowly.

"Yes, my sweet girl, this is where you belong. Karissa, worshipping your pussy while I worship your mouth with my cunt. So fucking perfect, my girls." She holds Adelaide's head in place as she tosses her head back with a moan.

I feel a thrill of happiness every time she calls us "hers" because I know that she means it. We are hers to enjoy, and she is ours to taste. Just as Adelaide is mine to enjoy and care for and I was hers to savor.

I increase my speed with my fingers and my mouth and I hold Adelaide in place as she lets out a muffled shout, her body writhing with her orgasm.

"Mmm, yes!" Josslyn cries softly, her own orgasm taking over her body.

After a few more seconds, I pull away, Josslyn following suit before reaching down to tangle her tongue with Adelaide's and then grabbing my face with a moan.

The taste of her pussy from Adelaide's lips, combined with the intoxicating taste of Adelaide's soaked slit, is almost too much. I echo her moan.

"I want to see Adelaide taste your sweet cunt, Karissa, but first I plan to take turns showing both of you exactly how I feel about your sweet pussies. You are both mine," she says softly before turning to capture Adelaide's lips again. I shudder in pleasure at her words.

She gets up from the couch, pulling us up before tugging us into a door we hadn't realized is at the far wall, near the kitchen. We follow her into her room where she points us to her bed. Following the unspoken command, we settle ourselves on her bed, while she adjusts her special strap-on. My mouth goes dry and my pussy aches as I take in the self-assured smirk on her face.

Suddenly, her wings burst out of her back, her horns on display as her tail swishes. Her claws, thankfully, aren't on display. "Both of you, on your knees, right next to each other," she says forcefully and we snap out of a haze and quickly do as she asks.

"I'm going to fuck both of you, but this time, I am going to give you the pleasure of my full powers," her voice growls out.

Lust pours through my body and Adelaide and I let out a crazed moan. My pussy drips down my thighs as Josslyn slams herself inside of me. I scream in pleasure.

"One of the benefits of being a Succubus is that, when I choose, I can control every bit of your pleasure. I can increase it, take it away, drive you mad with lust or give you the most powerful orgasm, over and over again until your body is spent." She works her hips and I feel an orgasm hit me, once, twice.

She laughs. "I can even make you feel as if I'm inside of you when I'm not. Isn't that right, Adelaide?"

Adelaide moans as she rocks her hips back and forth, as if she is being fucked.

She pulls out of me and moves over to slam into Adelaide, rocking her body as Adelaide moans in pleasure. "I can even make you feel my mouth if I choose too."

I gasp as I still feel her thrusting inside of me as if she never stopped. Except now, I feel her lips and tongue running up and down my slit as she takes my clit into her mouth. I feel her hands pinch my nipples even though they are firmly wrapped around Adelaide's waist as she fills her up.

Adelaide cries out, "Yes, yes. So good. Your mouth is so good."

I moan wildly as another orgasm is ripped out of my body. I feel my body shudder as Josslyn laughs, the sound breathless as her own orgasm shoots through her.

She moans. "The best part is that every time you come for me, my own power increases and the longer I can go, making sure both of you are completely satisfied. *This* is what it means to be mine. My protection, my obsession, your ongoing pleasure, and happiness." She moves inside of Adelaide more rapidly, punctuating her point with her thrusts.

The feeling echoes inside of me as if she is fucking me too. Her phantom mouth continues to drive my pussy and breasts crazy. I feel another orgasm rip through me and I almost sob as my body shakes.

"You two are fucking mine even when you see another patron. Even when you taste each other, every night. Even when Karissa fucks your sweet face with her pussy, Adelaide, or Karissa wraps her perfect lips around your plump pussy, making you come for her, like the good girl you are. You are both mine." She smacks Adelaide's ass, and her phantom hands slap mine. She pulls out of Adelaide and pushes inside of me with a deep moan. Collecting some of my juices, she swirls one finger and then two into my tight rim and I shout at the strange but mind-blowing sensation as I feel the pressure of her "dick" and her fingers at the same time.

"Fuck yes. Fuck my ass," Adelaide shouts, her body shaking with another orgasm.

Josslyn chuckles as the pressure increases. "Yes, I own your bodies and you both will own mine. Now come for me."

My body does as she commands immediately, as wave after wave of pleasure crashes over me.

She pulls out and kneels in front of us." Both of you lick yourselves off me." We run our lips and tongue up and down her strap-on, moaning breathlessly while she continues to fuck our dripping cunts, asses and her mouth works us over.

"My sweet girls, so perfect and mine, all fucking mine," she says gently, her gaze dropping to our faces, a soft expression on her face.

All yours, I think to myself as another orgasm rips through my body.

The End...For Now

Want to see whose story is next? Turn the page.

Coming Soon
Bethany

Bethany always did everything she was supposed to do. Get perfect grades, and be the perfect daughter She even married at the ridiculous request of her father just so he would release her trust fund so she could start her own business.

Bethany needed the freedom of making her own choices, her life, beige, and monotone.

That is until her internship introduced her to a place where she could live out her deepest desires. After her boss got her into the city's most infamous and exclusive club, she realized it was much more than a club for the rich a powerful.

No, Femme Fatale was a club for women, by women.

Being given the chance to be taken on as a patron despite the apparent years-long wait list, Bethany learns about herself in the sweetest ways.

With the help of Fatale's Caterina, Jaime, and Rachel, Bethany learns how to give up control and let someone else take the reins. In doing so, Bethany learns that sometimes being at the mercy of someone, or rather, certain someone can be a good thing.

Welcome to Femme Fatale the Cast is ready to welcome you.

Introducing The Cast

Josslyn- Owner, Dominant, Succubus

Karissa- Dom/Sub Fatale

Adelaide- Submissive Fatale

Jaime- Freshly auditioned new Dominant member of Femme Fatale

Chloe- Bartender, Fatale

Trisha- Dominant Fatale

Caterina- Dominant Fatale

Rachel- Sub/Dom Fatale

Leija- Dominant Fatale who specializes in pain

Mrs. Vance- Submissive customer, works exclusively with Leija, Trisha, Caterina, and now Jaime

Mrs. Janet- Dominate customer -works with Karissa and Adelaide-

Myia Day- Customer who likes variety and will work exclusively with Jaime, Adelaide and Karissa

Bethany- Submissive, no pain. Discovering her sexuality will work with Caterina, Jaime, and Rachel.

Acknowledgments

To my Keyboard Whores…This is our time to shine.

Ruby curses a bit too much, moms a bit too hard, and loves her husband with everything she is. Even more so, she loves all her characters because, in some aspects, they are a small representation of who Ruby is; bold, unapologetic, and accepting of her sexuality and all of her desires. She has never been able to do anything without being considered a bit TOO MUCH. But that is okay because there is never such a thing as too much love (for oneself or others), too much sex, or too much support for her friends and family.

Oh, Ruby is also a bit of a smut enthusiast and proud of it.

Printed in Great Britain
by Amazon